R.J. SIERRA

WORLD ON FIRE

aethonbooks.com

The ground shook fiercely at my command, and a fissure opened up in the middle of my jail cell. I dove into it, disappearing into the ground like a swimmer leaping into the churning sea.

This, I could have done without lifting a finger.

Another time, instead of an earthquake, I reached deep into the walls of the cell, using my control of all things rock and stone to blow apart the cinder blocks. Dusting myself off, I stepped through the hole in the wall and walked off into the night as if I'd never been imprisoned for a murder I hadn't committed.

This, too, I could have done with minimal effort.

Taking another tack, I channeled ley line energy from the ground, bringing up great crackling bolts of it to fill the air and electrify the bars of my cell. When guards touched the bars, they were shocked unconscious. The charge was so strong, it sprang the lock on the door of my cell, opening it before me.

Again, this could have been easily done.

For I, Gaia Charmer, am the human avatar of Mother Earth herself. No jail cell can long resist my power...the power of a planet at my fingertips.

So why, with all I could do, was I still sitting in the cell at the police station in Confluence, Western Pennsylvania instead of running free to track down the killer whose crimes I'd been blamed for?

Let's just say I play by the rules. Though I was starting to wonder, with the way things were going, if that was about to change.

"How are you doing, Gaia?" Sheriff Dale Briar walked up to the bars and gazed in at me with his bright hazel eyes. "Can I get you anything?"

I sat on a bench along the wall of the cell, staring back at him, and shook my head slowly. It was still hard to believe that we were on opposite sides of the bars. Looking out from inside a jail cell at the man who was my boyfriend was something I'd never expected.

I hadn't gotten any more used to it in the hour since he'd brought me in, either. I still couldn't wrap my head around the fact that Sheriff Briar, who'd never seemed to doubt me for a second in all the time we'd been together, had marched me out of my offices at Cruel World Travel/Charmer Investigations and locked me in a holding cell at the local police station.

"When can I get out of here?" I leaned forward on the bench, nervously twisting the blonde braid that lay over my right shoulder. "When can I go home?"

"Duke and Luna just asked me the same question." Briar hiked a thumb at the door behind him that led to the squad room. "I still don't have a good answer."

"Are you going to charge me, or what?" I asked.

Briar pulled out his phone. "I'm not sure what to do at this point, to be honest."

"You *know* I didn't kill Imogene Parker." I got up from the bench and walked over to him. "No matter what the evidence says."

I knew it hadn't looked good for me from the start. The 85-year-old had suffocated after being pumped full of dirt, and a note left at the murder scene had pointed a finger in my direction.

Mother Earth is coming for the wicked, it had said.

Not to mention, Imogene was the second elderly woman in town to die under the same circumstances in a matter of days—stuffed with dirt, accompanied by a cryptic note that mentioned Mother Earth.

And then there was the *other* old woman, the one buried under crushed cinderblocks in the basement of Imogene's house. The one who'd personally identified me as Imogene's murderer once I'd set her free.

It hadn't looked good for me from the start...so how on Earth could it possibly look any worse?

"I need to show you something." Briar held up the phone so I could see the video playing on its screen. From a high camera angle looking down on Imogene's living room, I clearly saw the old lady sitting in a recliner, watching TV.

Then, by the flickering light of the TV, I saw someone enter the room and attack. The scene was grainy and dark, but I could still see the attacker as she went to work on Imogene...especially when she glowed with radiant energy and summoned streams of dirt through the window to fill up the old lady's throat.

It was then, plain as day, that I could see the attacker looked just like *me*. She was slender and petite, in her mid-20s, with long blonde hair pleated into a ponytail draped over one shoulder. She even wore a leather jacket like mine with a black top and black jeans underneath.

"That's impossible," I said in a hushed voice. "I was at the Council of Landkind meeting, and then I was at the office..."

"According to Dr. Cox, the murder happened the night before." Briar switched off the video and slipped the phone back in the pocket of his uniform pants. "So where were you two nights ago, Gaia?"

The question stung. "You don't think I *did* this, do you?"

"Of course not," said Briar. "I'm sure you didn't...but I have to ask. If you have an alibi, I need to know what it is."

I scowled at him. "Either you believe me or you don't, Briar. I don't need to explain my whereabouts."

"Gaia, listen." He leaned toward me, locking his grim gaze with mine. "I'm being straight with you here. You don't need to convince *me*, but..." He drew a long breath and let it out slowly. "Between the video I just showed you, and the one from the doorbell cam, and Beatrice Brown's identifying you as the killer....it looks bad. There's so much here, I can't just make it go away, as much as I want to."

A sick feeling crawled through me as I heard those words. The way he'd said them, there hadn't been much hope in his voice.

"Gaia." Briar reached between the bars, took my hands in his, and lowered his voice. "There must be another explanation for this."

He was right, but I couldn't think what it might be. I just stared down at his hands, wondering how we'd gotten to this terrible place.

"You've been through some crazy stuff, just since I've known you," said Briar. "Could this be part of all that? Some enemy masquerading as you? Someone with the same powers, able to make themselves look just like you?"

I shrugged. My memories of my current and past incarnations had never been perfect—and, lately, I'd realized they were even more unreliable than I'd thought. If a likely culprit could be found somewhere in my many long lives, I couldn't remember them…and maybe I never would.

For now, I was just as much in the dark as Briar was and facing a challenge for what might have been the first time in my existence.

I, the planet Earth in human form, was being framed for murder.

"Keep thinking," said Briar. "Because the truth is, this situation might be out of my hands."

I nodded, understanding what he was telling me. Completely comprehending the words he'd left unsaid.

"I'm slow-walking the process," he said. "I haven't charged you yet, and I've filed no paperwork. But I'll have to, sooner or later. I'll have to take a statement from Beatrice Brown in the hospital, and I'll have to interrogate you formally. I'll have to do everything by the book, understand?"

He squeezed my hands tightly, and I nodded again.

"But I'm not stupid enough to think I can figure out this mess and deliver any kind of justice to anyone." Briar narrowed his eyes as he kept his gaze locked with mine. "There's only one person in the world who can do all that, I think."

I knew exactly who he was talking about, and it scared me. Because that person had a terrible task ahead, one that might very well lead them to some very dark places.

And that person was me.

"Gaia…honey…" Briar squeezed my hands even tighter. "I can see how this is going to go. I can see it a mile away. I don't know why it's happening, and I don't know who's responsible…but I can see the writing on the wall." He lowered his voice to a whisper. "And

I want you to know, Gaia, whatever you end up doing, I won't hold it against you."

A chill shot me through me as I realized what had just happened. As Briar released my hands and backed away, watching me with eyes glistening as if he might never see me again.

He'd given me permission. That was what he'd done.

He'd given me permission to do what I needed to do to save myself.

I kept thinking there must be another way. After all, I was completely innocent; together, we had to be able to get to the truth and clear my name.

But in my heart, I knew better. In my heart, I already knew damn well what I was going to have to do.

"Thank you." So that was what I told him. "Thank you for everything."

Briar nodded. "All in a day's work, ma'am." And then he smiled that wide-open smile of his, the one that had made me fall in love with him in the first place. The one that had made my love feel bigger than the world, more important than anything in it…at least for a while.

Then he opened the door to the squad room and stepped through it, looking back over his shoulder as he went. "Duke and Luna are still out here, wanting to see you. Okay if I send them back?"

"Sure," I said. "But I guess we'd better keep it short, huh?"

"Up to you." He shrugged. "Though I must admit, it's getting kind of late."

With that, he was gone, leaving me standing alone in my cell, feeling more trapped than I could ever remember feeling, even though I had the powers of a planet and my boyfriend's permission to escape before the whole world came crashing down around me.

My heart beat faster when my best friend and my sister entered the room—even as I tried not to think about the fact that this might be the last time I ever saw either of them.

"Earth Angel." Duke, who'd been my guide and satellite throughout my current incarnation, shook his head in sadness and rage. "I still can't believe this. It simply isn't *possible*."

"Yet here I am." I spread my arms and smiled, trying to hide my deep sadness. "Mother Earth, in a cage."

"We know you don't belong here." Luna Neil, my sister, is the avatar of the moon. In my current incarnation, I'd only met her recently, before the war with the Allself and Terralyzers…but the bond between us was strong. "We won't let you be punished for something you didn't do."

"Tell that to my identical twin," I said. "The one who killed Imogene Parker in the video. The one Beatrice Brown met face-to-face at the murder scene before she was buried alive."

"Don't worry, we'll find her." Luna's pale gray eyes glinted. "We've already put the word out, and the search is underway."

Duke nodded. "The Council of Landkind has issued a warrant for her arrest. Every landform in the area and beyond is looking for this vile imposter."

"That's good to know," I told him. Landkind were the human avatars of landforms—valleys, rivers, mountains, lakes—and they could search with the senses of the land and its elements as well as with those of humans. They could cover a lot of ground, in other words.

But I didn't get my hopes up. My double had gone to a lot of trouble to frame me. I couldn't imagine finding her would be all that easy.

"Do you have *any* idea who she is?" asked Luna. "Some kind of a shapeshifter, maybe? An agent of the Allself, or one of the escaped hybrids from Parapets?"

"Someone who looks just like me and has the same power over the Earth?" I shook my head. "Not a clue."

"Earth Angel, I've been thinking." Duke narrowed his eyes and lowered his voice. "What if she's a *golem*?"

He'd surprised me, though I was sure the notion had come naturally to him. After all, Duke was a golem himself, a creature of earth and magic animated by the spirit of the late, great jazz musician and bandleader, Duke Ellington.

"I don't know," I told him. "I guess it's possible."

Luna, short and squat as she was, looked moonlike as she stood there, shaking her head. "If that's the case, this is worse than we thought. A golem can just fall apart into dirt and mud, right? There might be only *one* Gaia Charmer to take the rap in the end."

"I'll bet I could handle it," Duke said darkly. "One golem to another."

"And then what?" I asked. "Get it to confess its crimes and its nature as a golem to a judge and jury?"

Duke thought for a moment, then grunted. "Damnit, Earth Angel. There has to be a way to get you out of this."

There was, but I didn't want either of them to know about it yet. The fewer people in the loop at that point, the better.

When I finally did what I had to do, I didn't want my friend and sister to pay the price for it.

"Listen," I told them. "The best thing you can do for me now is take care of yourselves and the businesses. Keep the town safe." I got choked up, then, and drew close to the bars. "I love you both, you know that?"

They closed in, too, each reaching out to take one of my hands. From the looks on their faces, I could see they were both deeply upset, worried what the future would bring. But did either of them have any idea this might be the last time we'd see each other?

As far as I could tell, I was the only one who had that idea.

"We love you too, sister," said Luna.

"On that, we can all agree." Duke smiled with all the charm he could muster, which was quite a bit for a golem created in the image of a charismatic 75-year-old musician.

"Give my best to Nephelae," I told them, referring to a nymph who owned an herb shop in town and was once of my closest friends. She hadn't been the same since she'd lost her lover, Minthe, in the battle with the Terralyzers. "Tell her to stay strong."

A single tear ran down Luna's cheek. "Leave it to you, sis. You're the one in trouble, and you're worried about other people."

We all fell silent then, caught in a moment frozen in time. It was the eye of a hurricane, a calm before the storm that was to come. Soon enough, it would sweep us all away, taking us far from this simple contact, this feeling of care and belonging.

Whatever was going to happen after that was anybody's guess.

Finally, I stood alone in my cell again, thinking about the task ahead. Briar had ushered out Duke and Luna, then closed the door to the squad room, leaving the holding cell quiet and still. No one remained to try to talk me out of anything, and there was no one to move me forward into the madness on the horizon.

Just me, and the walls, and the bars.

In other words, the time was perfect for what I needed to do.

Standing in the middle of the cell, I closed my eyes and spread my arms wide. I reached out with my mind, as I always did when touching the world around me—the planet with which I was so inextricably linked.

Focusing my will, I reached for the substance and soul of the Earth, trying to make contact. Once I connected, I could make the rock and dirt and power of the world obey me, breaking me out of my cell with a fissure or earthquake or electrical storm. It was a boundless source of strength, a reservoir of might that had seen me through terrible struggles and freed me from inescapable traps.

But not this time.

I reached and found nothing. I called, and there was no reply. It was as if the entire world had gone dead around me.

Grimacing, I tried again, redoubling my effort. I strained with every iota of will at my command, digging deeper, ever deeper.

Still, I was cut off. The Earth, which had always been an extension of myself, was closed to me.

Heart pounding with panic, I fell to my knees. Maybe, if I just got closer to the ground under the floor, I could find the spark that eluded me.

Hands pressed to the cement, I scrambled to tap the light within the earth…but found only darkness. It was like suddenly being blind, unable to see the vast world around me though I knew it was there.

All those visions of escape I'd had—they were lost to me now. The Earth that I'd known so well and touched so easily with my mind and soul was just a memory. The planet might as well have been gone altogether for all that I could make contact with it.

As far as I was concerned, there was just a hole where the world had been, a dark gulf that gave nothing back though I poured everything I had into it.

"No!" I slumped on my side on the cold cell floor, curling up in a fetal position. "Please, no!"

Maybe I shouldn't have been surprised. Weeks ago, during the war with the Allself and the Terralyzers, my powers had been on the fritz, fading and returning unexpectedly.

But the loss had never been this complete. Even when my powers had been on the wane, my connection to the Earth had not been severed to this extreme.

Now, it was like someone had flipped a switch, and everything that was special about me had gone away. Along with my hope of escape.

Without my powers, I was truly trapped. I was at the mercy of the justice system, caught in a web of seemingly incontrovertible proof.

And meanwhile, as I cried on the floor, a fake Gaia was out there somewhere, no doubt hard at work doing even more damage to my good name.

And *she* was the one with the powers.

What now? I wondered. *What happens now?*

Moments later, I had my answer.

That was when the chips of cinderblock started popping out of the wall of my cell.

3

Chik chik chik

Jumping to my feet, I backed up against the bars, expecting the wall to cave in. Expecting, perhaps, my murderous doppelgänger to charge through and finish me off.

But nothing of the sort happened. The chips of beige-painted cinderblock just kept popping out of the wall and peppering the floor, a few at a time. For no discernible reason, they just kept coming.

Chik chik

Frowning, I walked closer, listening for some sign of what was causing the phenomenon. Still, all I heard was the clicking of the chips on the cement floor.

There was a window in that wall, but it was cut too high for me to look out and down. The cell was at street level, so there could very well be someone out there in the alley, but I couldn't get a look at them.

Briefly, I thought about calling for Briar, but decided against it. I seriously doubted Dark Gaia was coming for me. As powerful as she was, flicking a few cinderblock chips at a time didn't seem like her style.

So who *was* out there doing that, then? At the rate they were going, it was going to take forever to find out.

Chik chik chik

I put my hands against the wall and reached out with my senses and mind, trying to feel my way through the cinderblock like I normally would. But my Mother Earth powers were still gone; no signal was getting through.

Chik chik chik

My only clue was that the cinderblock chips were popping free in a roughly circular area near the floor, about three feet in diameter, a little to the left of the window. The rest of the wall was intact as ever; only that one circle was losing substance.

Chik chik chik chik chik

Suddenly, the rate of chipping increased, and I yanked my hand away. More and bigger chips popped free of the block and scattered on the floor, accumulating quickly in a layer of beige bits. Somehow, the process was picking up speed and force.

Chik chik chik chik chik chik chik

Clunk

Just as I stepped aside, the biggest chunk yet flew out, a piece about the size of my hand...then another. More chunks and chips followed, leaving the circular area more and more pitted.

Chik chik chik chunk

It was then that spots of light from the alley outside showed up on the floor. Whoever was working their way through the wall, they'd finally broken through.

"Who's out there?" I leaned down, still staying off to the side, and called into the opening. "Who are you?"

"Damnit!" The voice was muffled. What I heard of it, I didn't recognize. "This is taking too long!"

"Hey!" I waved my hand in front of the gap. "I asked who's there."

"Stay back!" hissed the voice. "I'm going to give it all I've got!"

Before I could do more than lean back a little from the opening, the remaining block in the circular section blew inward, blasting shards of wall through a cloud of dust.

Coughing, I batted at the billowing cloud, staring in the direction of the hole in the wall. Little by little, I was able to see it as the dust cleared—imperfect, ragged-edged, smaller than I'd expected... but a way out.

"Come on!" said the voice. "Hurry!"

I glanced over my shoulder. No one was on the other side of the bars yet, but the noise would bring someone soon. Even if Briar dragged his feet on my behalf, he couldn't ignore the ruckus for long.

"Let's go!" snapped the voice.

I dropped to my hands and knees in front of the hole. It would be a tight fit, but I thought I could just make it.

Still, I hesitated. Once I crossed that threshold, there would be no turning back.

Not to mention, I had no idea who was waiting for me on the other side or what was in store for me. All that lay in that direction was the great unknown.

Though it was true, all that lay in the other direction was seemingly ironclad evidence and an open-and-shut case against me. I couldn't see any clear path to freedom if I stayed.

But the hole in the wall was another story.

Sucking in my breath, I zipped up my leather jacket and pushed myself into the opening. The broken edges of the cinderblocks dug through the jacket into my shoulders and belly as I took hold of the outside rim and dragged myself forward.

But then, when I was halfway out, I got stuck. As petite as I was, I still couldn't quite make it.

Grunting, I twisted in the hole, fighting to force my way through. At any moment, I expected someone inside the building to grab my legs and haul me back through into the cell.

Instead, my rescuer in the alley suddenly seized my hands and wrenched me free. I lurched forward, landing on my elbows on the pavement.

The rest of my body slid out after me, and I rolled over on my back. It was then, as I looked up, that I finally saw who was behind my prison break.

"When did the Earth get to be such a fat-ass?" A woman gazed down at me, looking sarcastic. Though her close-cropped hair was black, the many wrinkles on her face told a different story about her age. "Never thought I'd have to tell a planet to go on a diet, but..."

"What's your name?" There was something familiar about her, but not familiar enough to recognize on the spot.

"Call me Mid." She reached down to help me up. "And enough

with the small talk. We gotta *bounce* before the *heat* comes down, honey."

As I got to my feet, I realized just how small Mid was, barely coming up to my breastbone. She was older than I'd thought at first, too. If I'd had to guess, I'd have said she was at least in her mid-80s.

This was my rescue party? Apparently so. Looking around, I saw no one else in the alley, waiting to do their bit.

"You're alone?" I frowned, starting to wonder if I'd made the right decision in coming this far. "Nobody's helping you?"

Without warning, she hauled off and smacked me in the chest. "Do I *look* like I need help?" She smacked me again. "You got a *problem* with me?"

I shook my head.

"Then let's stop standing around wasting time!" She started down the alley, hobbling fast, and waved for me to follow.

As I followed, her hobble became a trot. She was in pretty good shape for someone in her 80s.

"I've got a car parked around the corner," she said. "And no, you can't drive it. Don't even think about it, sweetheart."

I stayed close, looking in every direction for signs of pursuit, listening for sirens. "Where are we going, anyway?"

"Someplace you haven't been in a hell of a long time," she snapped. "And neither have I."

I scowled. "Where's that?"

"There's a whole *world* beyond *this* shithole," said Mid. "Let's go see if you still recognize it."

4

It was almost midnight, and the offices of Cruel World Travel/Charmer Investigations were still brightly lit and crowded with people.

As Mid drove past on the way out of town, I got a good look at the place, peering through the rear passenger's side window while trying not to make myself too visible. I knew I was taking a risk, but I had to do it.

For all I knew, this might be the last time I saw the place or any of the people inside.

Mid slowed down the slightest bit as we passed, just enough to let me take it all in. I asked her to slow the silver Toyota Corolla even more or just stop, it wouldn't attract attention…but she ignored me and kept rolling at the same speed.

So I took what I could get. Through the office front windows, I watched the crowd—the Council of Landkind—as they shouted at each other, arguing passionately. Fingers were pointed, voices were raised, fists were pounded on desks.

Given the circumstances and the lateness of the hour, I thought I could guess what they were fighting about in there. I didn't have to read lips to know they were trying to decide what to do about me and my arrest.

If I could have told them about the breakout, it would've changed the whole direction of the meeting.

"I hate to just leave them like this." My heart pounded as I said those words. "They're my friends."

"Oh boo hoo," said Mid. "You're on the lam now, honey. This is how it works."

As I watched, Ashanti raised her hands over her head and shouted for attention, calming the crowd. She made a grim statement, and then Duke joined in, and Nephelae said something, too.

We were just about past the building when the door swung open, and Luna looked out. Her eyes fixed on our car, following it as it drifted up the street…and for a moment, I could've sworn she looked right at me.

But then, she turned to look in the other direction, down the street, and the moment of imagined contact was gone. Disappointment washed over me as the distance between us grew. As the distance between *all* of us grew.

Would I ever see any of them again? Or were they gone, and my old life over for good?

As just another person, a woman with no more power over the Earth than any human being off the street, I wasn't confident that I'd ever make my way back there again. But maybe, someday, I could still make contact again, even if it was just over the phone or by letter.

And maybe then, I could thank them for their love, apologize for leaving the way I did, and tell them one more thing besides all that.

Maybe then, I could finally tell them goodbye.

5

Mid drove west along the Pennsylvania Turnpike, squinting into the darkness from behind her gold wire-framed spectacles. Leaning forward, she looked for all the world like just another old lady at the wheel—but her hands were steady, and her technique was sound. The Corolla sailed down the road at a constant speed, never swimming in the lane or veering from oncoming traffic. As unsettled as I felt given the craziness in my life, I never for a second felt uncertain about the old woman's command of the vehicle.

Everything else about Mid was still a question mark, though… and so far, she hadn't volunteered to fill in the blanks. In fact, she seemed perfectly content to drive on in silence, keeping her secrets to herself.

Somewhere past Pittsburgh, though, as we rolled toward the border of Ohio, I decided it was finally time to get some answers.

"So, who are you, Mid?" I narrowed my eyes as I stared at the little old lady in the driver's seat. "How did you manage to take down the wall of my jail cell?"

"I'm like you," said Mid. "You, the way you *used* to be, anyway."

"The way I *used* to be?"

"Before you lost your *powers*, honey." Mid flickered her fingers on the steering wheel. "Back in the good old days of a couple *hours* ago."

I frowned, trying to parse what she'd just told me. "You're Land-kind, then?"

"Nope." Mid shook her head.

"A Groundswell Crossbreed? A Terralyzer?"

Mid clucked in dismissal. "You think too small."

My frown deepened. "A goddess, maybe? A nymph or a Hyade?"

"Try an actress." Mid shrugged. "And a singer. Though those days are long gone now for me."

We slowed down for a toll booth, then, and I waited until we were through it to keep up the questioning. "An actress?" Something about what she'd said had set off alarm bells in my mind. "What name did you go by?"

"The same one I was given at birth." She glanced over and gave me a quick wink. "Mid Silvergone."

When I heard the full name, a light bulb went off in my head. Finally, I knew why she'd seemed so familiar.

When Ellie Grenoble, another elderly resident of Confluence, had been killed—murdered the same way Imogene Parker had been, suffocated with dirt—she'd left behind three full scrapbooks in her home. One of them had featured page after page of photos and clippings recounting the career of the one and only Mid Silvergone, whom I'd never heard of before.

Only now, she was right there beside me, steering into the night —and she apparently had powers like the ones I'd had most of my life.

"I still don't understand," I said. "How did you get to be how I used to be?"

"Oh, you know." Mid glanced at me sideways. "Girl sponta-neously comes to life with a physical age of 22. Girl discovers she's Mother Earth in human form. Girl manifests powers to control the substance and forces of the planet."

I reeled as her words sank in. "You're telling me you're an *avatar* of the world like I am?"

"Correct."

"But that's not possible. Earth's avatars never *overlap*."

"Bullshit," snapped Mid. "Who says so?"

"It's what I was taught." Duke, my personal "moon" and

guardian, had done the teaching, but I left him out for now. "The old avatar leaves before the new one arrives in the world."

"Then how come *I* never left?" asked Mid.

"Maybe you're not who you say you are," I suggested. "Maybe you just have a line of B.S. and some tricks up your sleeve."

Mid chuckled. "You know who I am, sweetheart? Who I *really* am? I'm one of the few people in the world who's on your side right now. Maybe the *only* one."

"Meaning what?" I wished I had my powers back, so I could force the car to stop and get the whole truth out of Mid. "What do you know about the woman who framed me for murder? Why did you break me out and help me get away?"

"Because the whole world is against you right now, or about to be," said Mid. "And if someone doesn't save *you*, then you can't save *them.*"

"Them who?" I asked, frustrated at the way she doled out bits and pieces of information. "Who am I supposed to *save?*"

Mid Silvergone cast a grim look across the seat, suffused with an eerie glow from the dim lights of the dashboard. For a moment, she looked like something much more than a little old lady with a bag of tricks.

"Humanity," she said coldly. "If you can't save them, they will be wiped from the face of the Earth very soon, and forever."

6

I didn't say anything for a while as Mid drove onward. I was lost in thought, processing what she'd said about the end of humanity.

Eventually, though, my reverie ended when she pulled over at a roadside rest stop. "Stay close," she said as we got out of the car. "If you sense anything suspicious, come and get me right away."

"Why?" I asked. "Is someone following us?"

Mid shrugged. "If not now, they will be soon. The whole *planet* will be hunting us."

"Because the whole planet wants to get rid of humanity?" I closed my door and followed her up the sidewalk toward the central building. "Are you sure? I was *one* with the Earth, and she *never* mentioned doing anything like that."

"Then maybe the Earth wasn't being up-front with you," said Mid. "And maybe there's a reason you've suddenly lost contact with the planet." She looked back at me with a grim expression. "Maybe she's keeping you out of the loop because she thinks you might try to *stop* her."

"That makes zero sense to me," I told her. "I *am* the planet. We are one and the same."

"Maybe things aren't quite as simple as you think," said Mid as she entered the building.

I hung back at the last second, letting the door close behind her.

23

It was then, standing outside by myself, that I thought about taking off to fend for myself.

It seemed like a great idea. I didn't like having my life and freedom in the hands of someone I hardly knew or trusted.

If I'd still possessed my powers, I wouldn't have thought twice about going off by myself. But without them, I faced a different calculation. If what she'd said about the whole world being against me was true, how could I stand on my own without a way to fight back?

Again, I tested my connection with the Earth, reaching into the network of ley line energy and geologic forces. Just like before, nobody answered my call, and I felt nothing. The planet was still a void to me, its multitude of miraculous qualities so unreadable that they might as well have been nonexistent.

Stepping off the sidewalk into the grass, I crouched and pressed both hands to the ground, trying once more to tune into the spark of the world. The result was the same as before.

As I got back to my feet, still bereft of my link with the Earth, I thought about running off into the woods anyway. Maybe the power loss was a temporary thing, and I'd be back to normal soon enough.

Or maybe it was permanent, and Mid Silvergone was my best chance at survival.

I sighed, thoroughly disgusted at the inevitable logic of my situation. As much as I wanted to go my own way, I knew I was better off staying the course…for now, at least.

"Damn." Shaking my head, I turned to enter the building…and stopped when I heard a sudden, loud rumbling from the grassy area where I'd just been crouching.

Looking back, I saw the ground falling inward, the green turf sliding into a central vortex like water down a drain. Another sinkhole opened up a few yards away, and another, each spinning to life in the grassy, flat ground most commonly used for picnics and walking dogs.

Heart hammering, I ran for the building. I burst through the door into the lobby, then charged into the women's bathroom after that. The whole time, I kept hearing the rumbling from outside.

"Mid!" I shouted.

She looked up from the sink, an expression of alarm crossing her features. "Shit." She ran from the sink, water still running, and bolted past me out the door.

As I followed her out of the building, I saw more sinkholes opening in the grass and sidewalk. When one crumbled directly in her path, she stopped and raised her hands, which were glowing brightly now. A fresh plug of sandstone surged up from the heart of the sinkhole at her command, filling the core even as more ground dropped away around it.

Seeing her in action made me wish more than ever that I had my powers back.

"Come on!" Walking as fast as she could, Mid skirted the edge of the plugged sinkhole, heading for the car. Even as I followed, a fresh pit fell open in the parking lot alongside us, and another consumed a stretch of sidewalk in our path.

Mid slipped between the latest holes, grabbing the car keys out of her purse. She used the remote to unlock the doors and start the engine.

As she pulled open the driver's side door, I ran to the passenger's side and leaped in. She was halfway in the car herself when the pavement under her started sinking into another hole.

Shooting across the seat, I grabbed her by the arms and hoisted her the rest of the way inside. Instead of stopping to thank me, she threw the car in reverse and stomped on the accelerator.

The Toyota burst backward just as the pavement crashed inward. Mid spun the wheel, whipping the car around, then threw it out of reverse and again stomped the pedal.

The driver's side door swung shut as the car flew forward. We blasted out of the rest stop and onto the interstate at a high rate of speed, escaping with our lives.

"So Mother Earth really is hunting me." Looking back, I saw walls and light poles collapsing as still more sinkholes fell open. "And she knows where I *am*."

"Not for long, with any luck." Mid kept racing through the night, pegging 90 on the speedometer. "She'll lose track if we keep moving. For a while, at least."

Eyes wide, I slumped in my seat. Things were worse than I'd imagined, now that I knew she'd told the truth. Not only had I been framed for murder by an identical twin...not only had I lost my powers and contact with the Earth…but now the planet and all her agents were out to kill me.

All because Mother Earth didn't want me to stop her from exterminating humankind.

"We don't have a chance, do we?" I said, staring at the dark pavement as it rolled toward us. "We can't possibly survive, let alone save the human race."

"Don't give up yet, honey," said Mid. "I've got a plan."

"What kind of plan?" I asked.

"A secret one," said Mid. "The kind that might just keep our asses out of the fire if we play our damn cards right."

"A secret plan," I said. "Secret even from me."

"For now." Mid looked over and smiled. "But you'll find out what it is soon enough."

"Well, I feel better already," I told her. "You're really filling me with confidence."

"How you feel doesn't matter," said Mid. "Just whether you're alive or not."

I folded my arms over my chest and stopped talking then, tired of her evasions…tired of everything. My whole life had turned to shit in the course of a day, and I was sick and tired of all of it.

I just wanted to go back to the way things were before. I just wanted to go home and be with Briar and Duke and Luna, to help people plan vacations at Cruel World Travel and track down bad guys through Charmer Investigations. I just wanted to feel the planet around me and know I was safe in its arms.

Then, for a little while, at least, I got my wish…at least in my dreams. As the car hurtled on through the night, I nodded off, dreaming about the life I'd left behind and might never be a part of again.

7

I woke from a deep sleep to find I was alone in the car. The driver's seat was empty, and the driver's side door was shut.

Heart pounding, I looked outside. Sometime during my nap, the dark of night had faded into predawn light, so I was able to get a good look at my surroundings.

I spotted Mid in a second, standing on the shore of a lake. The car was parked in a lot a little way back, nose toward the water.

Frowning, I opened the door and got out. There was the slightest chill in the air as I walked across the grass, passing a large sign warning that the lake was off-limits to swimmers and fishermen due to high levels of contamination.

Without a word, I joined Mid on the pebbled bank, staring out over the water as it lapped at the stones not far from our feet.

"It's coming." She nodded at the brightening sky beyond the far rim of the lake. "And it's gonna be a good one."

I fixed my gaze on the brightest patch of sky, where the sun was getting ready to poke its way up over the horizon. Ribbons of cloud drifted near the spot, already turning pink as the light intensified.

"Are we okay here?" I asked. "Can she find us like she did at the rest stop?"

"It's a bit of a dead zone because of all the pollution in the lake. The more contaminated the environment, the harder it is for

Mother Earth to see through the impurities." Mid shrugged. "But who knows?"

"Well, that's comforting."

"Until yesterday, you were one of Earth's avatars," said Mid. "Even without your powers, you probably stick out like a sore thumb."

"Is that what I was?" I asked. "Not Mother Earth herself?"

"An avatar, yes," said Mid. "An instrument, channeling the power and awareness of the Earth. You might even have thought you *were* her, and you were, in a way—but only one fragment, one sliver of her consciousness."

I shook my head slowly. "But I thought…it felt so…"

"I know." Mid smiled. "It felt so *true*. That's how it works, until something like this happens, and she cuts you off…or, in your case, sets out to destroy you."

A light breeze fluttered my bangs, and I suddenly felt hopelessly doomed. How long could I possibly survive with the planet and all her resources in pursuit with my trail so easy to track?

"Maybe I should just go back to Confluence," I said. "At least I have friends there."

"I wouldn't bet the farm on that." Mid looked at me sideways. "Remember, you have an evil twin on the loose."

"Shit." My stomach twisted painfully. I hadn't thought about it until now…but *of course* my people at home were in danger. "Now I want to go back even *more*."

"*This* is your road, Gaia." Mid pointed at the ground under our feet. "The only road where humanity has the *slightest* chance. And *this* road doesn't go back."

We stood silently for a moment as the sky continued to brighten, the ribbons of cloud turning a bolder shade of pink. When was the last time I'd watched a sunrise in person? I couldn't remember.

"So, tell me," I said. "Why exactly is humanity on the chopping block? Why does the Earth want to wipe them out?"

"Why do you think?" asked Mid. "It's *her* or *them* these days, isn't it? It's a matter of *survival*."

I nodded slowly, watching as the sky brightened even more. It wouldn't be long now until the sun itself appeared in all its glory.

"Couldn't she reverse climate change, though? Couldn't she restore the environment to a pristine state?"

"Over time, maybe," said Mid. "If people wise up and cease their destructive ways. But what are the chances of that?"

The chances were slim, and I knew it.

"She's fighting for survival, Gaia. Can you blame her?"

"Whose side are you on, anyway?" I asked.

Mid thought for a moment. "Both." She looked at me, then back at the sunrise. "But humanity needs help more than the planet right now. Mother Earth has the upper hand."

"How so?"

"Her *war-self* has broken free," Mid said darkly. "Her avatar of unchecked power and limitless cruelty. The part of her that exists only to destroy that which would otherwise destroy her."

I frowned. "Why haven't I heard of this war-self before now?"

"Good question," said Mid.

Just then, the sun burst over the horizon, its blinding streamers blazing against the bright blue sky. The pink ribbons of cloud took on a golden hue, and a streak of reflected light flared over the rippling water like a road leading right to us.

In that moment, gazing at the sky as I stroked my pleated braid, I was caught up in the dazzling display. I couldn't look away or think of anything else.

Though I was cut off from my powers and unable to connect to the Earth as an avatar, I marveled at the beauty before me. If anything, I felt a deeper appreciation of the scenic grandeur *because* I couldn't connect with its source. I was forced to take it all in as a normal human might, relying on five senses with no enhancement or superhuman boost.

In that way, I had an entirely new experience, appreciating the beauty of the sunrise purely on a surface level. I wasn't, at the same time, listening to the groaning of the Earth or the cries of the beasts or the multitude of physical processes occurring all around me at any given second.

There was just the sun, its golden light streaming through the sky, painting a masterpiece that varied from moment to moment.

I loved it with all my heart. For the first time since my powers had left me, I didn't miss them.

"Nothing like a good sunrise to start your day off right, huh?" Mid spread her arms wide. "Good to see the world's still turning."

"Not bad," I said, but I couldn't help wondering, even as I admired the beauty arrayed before me, if it might be the last sunrise I'd ever see.

8

After sunrise, we got back in the car and continued down a winding two-lane road. When Mid started yawning, I offered to take the wheel…but she wouldn't hear of it. She knew best where we were going, she said, and could get us there fastest. Besides, she said, she had a sense of when Mother Earth was zeroing in on us and the heat was on. She would be quickest to react, she assured me.

Nevertheless, I tried to keep her talking—and therefore, awake and alert.

"You still haven't told me where we're going," I said. "Or what exactly the plan is—the one that's supposed to keep our asses out of the fire."

"Don't worry," she told me. "You'll see when we get where we're going."

I looked over at her then, feeling annoyed. It shouldn't have been difficult to get a little old lady like her to spill her guts—but I already knew she had more powers than I did. Powerless as I was, I didn't dare move against her, in spite of my desperate need for answers.

"I'd like to know what to expect." Trying to talk her into dishing was the best I could manage. "I've had enough surprises to last me a while."

Hands locked at ten and two o'clock on the wheel, she didn't take her eyes off the road. "I'm hungry," she said. "I could go for some breakfast."

A billboard advertising a diner loomed large and slid past. For the first time, I realized we were in the state of Indiana. *Indiana's Finest Diner,* said the tagline on the sign. The actual restaurant was called the Double D Diner.

"Whatever you want." I sighed. "Apparently, I'm just along for the ride, anyway. I have no real say in what happens next."

"Sure you do." She smirked. "I promise, you can tell the waitress just how you like your coffee and if you want your eggs dippy or scrambled."

I scowled, thinking again about jumping ship. In spite of the obvious consequences, the idea of going home to face the music still had its appeal.

"Double D Diner it is." Mid flicked on her turn signal, though the diner was still a mile up the road. "What's that?" She cupped her right ear with one hand and leaned toward me. "Breakfast is your treat, you say?"

"If I didn't just break out of jail and had some *cash* in my pocket, maybe." I wagged my head in disgust. "And if you gave me a *clue* to what your plan is."

"Be sure to eat up," said Mid as the diner drew nearer. "I don't intend to stop for lunch if I can avoid it."

"That depends on if the food is edible," I told her. "The place looks like kind of a dump from here, I've gotta say."

"It *is* a dump," she said as we pulled into the gravel parking lot. "Why do you think we're stopping here? The more toxic the environment, the less Mother Earth can see into it, remember?"

As we sat in a corner booth and pored over a pair of stained paper menus, the Double D sweltered and sizzled around us. The place smelled like frying onions, and everything looked about fifty years old. The red vinyl benches in the booth were as cracked and lumpy as the red stools along the counter. Instead of air conditioners, a couple of weathered and wobbly ceiling fans batted at the thick, dusty air, barely eking out a breeze.

The only other customers were an elderly couple at a table on the far side of the place and a trucker type at the counter in a wifebeater t-shirt, faded jeans, and dirty black Mac Truck ball cap. I didn't think I was going out on a limb when I guessed the big red pickup out front belonged to him.

All three of them seemed content to leave us alone so far. Only the waitress, a middle-aged woman in a tattered peach uniform and cap, was giving us the time of day…and that, just to take our orders.

The name on her nametag was Gertie. "Okay, got it." She finished scribbling on her order pad and read back what she'd written for Mid. "One number three, over easy, with home fries, rye toast, and a side of scrapple." Mid nodded, and Gertie turned to me. "One order of French toast with a side of bacon. That it?"

"Yes, thanks," said Mid.

"All righty then." Gertie smiled. "I'll be right back with more coffee lickety split."

With that, she hurried behind the counter and pushed her way through the swinging door to the kitchen.

Leaning back on my seat, I took another look around the place. The more grease and grime I saw, the more I lost my appetite. I seriously thought it might have been decades since the last time the Double D had been thoroughly cleaned.

"The Earth doesn't need to try to kill us in here," I said. "The food will take care of that."

"Beggars can't be choosers." Mid had a swallow of coffee from her chipped white cup. "And besides, we're not really here for the food anyway."

I frowned and sat up straight. "Don't tell me it's because of the ambience."

"We're meeting someone." Mid sipped more coffee. "An old friend of mine."

Just then, Gertie returned with a fresh pot of coffee and filled our cups. "This oughtta wake you gals up. And your food is on the way."

We thanked her, she left, and I pulled Mid's refilled cup away from her. "What old friend are we meeting?" I asked. "And why are we meeting her?"

"Relax, he's on your side." Mid pulled the cup back and hit it with cream and sugar. "One of the few."

Suddenly, the door jingled open, and a tall man in a state police uniform entered. He had broad shoulders and long legs and looked like he could have been in his late 20s or early 30s.

I tensed up, instantly nervous. I was wanted for murder and couldn't afford to let anyone take me in.

But then the trooper headed straight for us, grinning. He took off his broad-brimmed hat, revealing close-cropped black hair underneath. There was no sign of aggressive behavior in his expression or any move he made.

"Hey there!" He stopped at our table, hat in hand, and smiled down at Mid, his dark brown eyes sparkling. "Long time no see, Mid Silvergone."

"Hey yourself, Ebon." Mid was tickled by the attention, her cheeks flushed. "Very glad you could make it." She gestured across the table in my direction. "This is Gaia Charmer. Gaia, this is Ebon James."

"I know that." Ebon reached down to shake my hand. "Your reputation precedes you, Ms. Charmer."

"As does the warrant for her arrest," whispered Mid. "Though I'm sure we can trust your discretion, Trooper James."

Ebon scowled at me for a moment. "Does a doodle bug dance on a dog's ass?" Then, the scowl became a smile, and he sat down on the bench beside Mid.

Mid chuckled. "I've missed you, Ebon." She put her hand on his arm. "The circumstances are lousy, but God, I'm glad to see you. It's been too long."

Ebon patted her hand affectionately. "It does seem like a hundred years ago since the *last* time we saved the human race."

A hundred years ago? My mind raged with questions as I stared at him, but then Gertie showed up with plates of food.

"Here ya' go, ladies." She slid the French toast in front of me and the number three with home fries, rye toast, and scrapple in front of Mid. "And what'll *you* have, handsome?" She pulled the order pad out of her apron pocket and licked the tip of her pencil. "Steak and eggs, maybe? That oughtta stick to your ribs."

"Perfect." Ebon grinned at her. "Can you make the steak a t-bone and give it to me well-done?"

"I can make it any bone you like, hon." Gertie winked before she turned and sauntered into the kitchen.

"Now that's what I call customer service," said Ebon when she'd gone.

Mid gave his arm a squeeze. "You still got it, Ebon. Good to know I can still count on *some* things in life."

"It's what I do." Ebon shrugged. "It's who I am."

Mid released his arm, picked up her fork and knife, and started working on her breakfast. "So have you given any thought to my proposal?"

"I'm here aren't I?" said Ebon. "I'm on board with the ultimate goal, as you know. But I can't deny I have my doubts about our chances."

Mid nodded. "It won't be easy fighting a planet. Especially with one of us powerless." She looked at me as she chewed a corner of rye toast.

"But our cause is just," said Ebon. "Saving billions of lives from extinction is a good thing."

"So how long do we have?" I asked.

Ebon frowned. "Until what?"

I shrugged. "It seems like we're in a hurry. When does time run out to save humanity?"

"We don't know, honey." Mid sipped her coffee. "But we don't think it will be long. The players are on the board, and the world is hunting us down. I don't think we'd be in the crosshairs already if we had lots of time until the extinction event."

I picked at my French toast, knowing I needed to eat though I had no appetite. "And what will that event be, exactly?"

"We don't know," said Mid. "Not yet, anyway."

"What *do* we know?" I asked.

"Not much," said Mid. "But enough. Enough to know we need to take drastic measures right now. Which is why Ebon is here."

"And what makes Ebon so special?" I asked.

"You'll see, hon." Mid jabbed Ebon in the side with her elbow and laughed. "Isn't that right, Eb?"

"Sooner or later." Ebon grinned. "But I promise, I'll do my level best not to let you down."

Staring hard, I wondered if I'd ever met him before. Something about him gave me a strange feeling. "You didn't answer my—"

"Order up!" Just then, Gertie marched out of the kitchen and plunked down a plate of steak and eggs in front of Ebon. "Just the way you like it, sweetheart. Well-done, like *everything* I do."

"This looks fantastic." Ebon unrolled the napkin from his place setting and pulled out the fork and knife. "I'll bet I don't even need a steak knife to cut that beauty."

"You could probably eat it with a spoon." Gertie leaned close and brushed a hand over his shoulder. "It's that tender, honey."

"I can't wait to dig in." This time, it was his turn to wink.

The cook rang the order bell in the kitchen, and Gertie had to go. She blew him a kiss as she walked away, looking like she'd gladly quit and do whatever he wanted if only he asked her.

"You love them all, don't you?" asked Mid.

"I cannot tell a lie." Ebon nodded as he cut a hunk of T-bone with his butter knife. "I do, at that."

As he and Mid chuckled, I dropped my fork on my plate of half-eaten French toast. The irresistible mystery trooper was getting on my nerves. Maybe fending for myself wasn't such a bad idea after all.

"Well, eat up, everyone." Mid dug another forkful of scrapple off her plate. "It's going to be a long haul from here…and it could get ugly, even with a police escort." She glanced out the window at Ebon's cruiser in the parking lot.

"I wonder how close the war bitch is." Ebon narrowed his eyes at me. "Can you tell? Can you get a vibe?"

I looked at him like he was crazy. "Why the hell would I be able to do that?"

"Why *wouldn't* you?" Smirking, he cut off another bite of steak, stacked some eggs under it on the fork, and slipped it all into his mouth.

I looked at Mid for an explanation, but she just waved for Gertie's attention. "Could we get a couple pieces of graham cracker pie over here?"

What wasn't she telling me? Maybe I had a better chance if I kept pressing Ebon. "Seriously." I locked my gaze with his. "Wouldn't we have a better chance at getting through this if I knew what the hell was going on?"

Ebon chewed and swallowed, his expression blank. He washed his food down with coffee, set the cup beside his plate, and pointed at the remains of my French toast with the tines of his fork. "Are you gonna finish that?"

At which point I threw myself back on the bench with arms crossed over my chest, sick and tired of being kept in the dark.

"Don't worry, sweetie," said Mid. "You'll know everything soon enough." She sighed, looking grim. "And then, trust me, you'll wish you didn't."

9

"Am I the person you're protecting, or am I your prisoner?"

I asked the question in the parking lot of the Double-D, after we'd walked out of the place. It occurred to me when I asked to borrow a phone, and Mid and Ebon both said no.

"You're definitely not a prisoner," said Mid.

"Then give me your phone." I snapped my fingers and extended a hand. "I need to call home and make sure everyone's all right."

"What would you do if they weren't?" asked Mid. "You're powerless."

"But you aren't, and maybe he isn't, either." I pointed at Ebon. "Whatever his deal is."

Ebon pulled a toothpick out of his mouth and poked it in my general direction, grinning. "You wouldn't believe it if I told you."

"I just need to know." Again, I snapped my fingers. "Please."

"You're a fugitive," said Mid. "Don't you think the authorities have bugged your office phones?"

The thought had occurred to me. "I need to know my friends are alive. Isn't there something we can do?"

We had just reached the Toyota when Ebon grabbed my hand. "Picture someone," he told me. "What they look like, what they sound like, where they are. See them clearly in your mind's eye."

I did as he said, closing my eyes and conjuring a lifelike image of my right-hand man, Duke. If some kind of magic was in play, he was the one I thought we'd have the most luck reaching.

Strange impressions flashed through my mind then, somehow provided by Ebon. I saw a dead deer along the side of a road…a shriveled gray tree without any leaves…a beekeeper's hive filled with motionless bees.

Then, suddenly, Duke's brown face swept into view in my mind, eyes shut…and his eyes shot open.

Earth Angel! His voice in my mind sounded as if he were right by my side. *Thank heaven!*

Duke! I framed each thought in my mind as if it were a prayer. *Are you all right? Is everyone okay?*

We are now. Duke's face frowned. *But we've had a most difficult night and morning since your jailbreak. Your duplicate paid us a visit at Cruel World/Charmer Investigations.*

What?!

At first, we thought she was you, said Duke. *She really is identical to you in every way.*

And then what? I asked, dreading the answer.

We realized who she was and tried to take her down, said Duke. *But she has all the powers you once had, and none of the restraint. She tore apart the office pretty well, I'm afraid.*

Please tell me no one was hurt!

Just a few scratches. The way he said it made me think he was downplaying the truth for my benefit. *And then she got away. She said she was coming after the real imposter, which I took to mean you.*

I breathed a sigh of relief that there had been no fatalities. Any alarm I felt over being pursued was nothing compared to that.

You should all be okay then, I said. *If the twin is on the move, Confluence is the best place for you to be.*

Like fun it is, snapped Duke. *You know damn well Luna and I should be at your side. As soon as we batten down the hatches here at the office, we're coming after you.*

No! I need you there right now!

Having us here won't do much good if you're dead, said Duke.

Please! I need you to stay right where you are.

Gaia, said Duke. *Are you still one with Mother Earth?*

I paused before answering. *You know I'm not.*

Then you realize we don't have to take orders from you anymore, don't you?

This isn't me giving an order, I told him. *I'm asking a favor. Please, stay put for now. I have a feeling I'll need your help there in Confluence before this is all over.*

Duke didn't answer for a moment, and I thought I might have lost the connection. Then, his voice full of disapproval, he spoke. *All right, Earth Angel. You win for now.*

Again, relief flowed through me. *Thank you, Duke. Thank Luna for me, as well.*

Don't thank her yet, said Duke. *I can't guarantee she'll do as you ask. That sister of yours is more strong-willed that I am, and that's really saying something.*

I smiled. *Just do the best you can with her, Duke. I know you'll manage.*

But what about you, Earth Angel? What are you going to do when that evil thing catches up?

Ebon squeezed my hand, signaling my call was at an end. I squeezed him back.

The same thing we always do, powers or not, I told him. *We're going to turn her world upside-down.*

For reasons that weren't explained to me, I was told to ride in the state police cruiser with Ebon while Mid piloted the Corolla on her own. Our two-car convoy rolled out of the Double-D parking lot, with the cruiser up front and the Toyota behind.

As we headed west, I got increasingly nervous. The diner had been a safe haven, free of attack, and now we were back on the open road again.

"Are you sure this is a good idea?" I asked Ebon. "Earth could launch an attack at any time out here, couldn't she?"

"She can try," he said, "but her accuracy might leave something to be desired."

I kept staring out the side window, watching for signs of an attack. "Why do you say that?"

"Because I'm here," said Ebon. "And I have a way of confusing things, especially where she's concerned."

I frowned, trying to understand. "Confusing things how?"

"I *blur* things," said Ebon.

"What things?"

"*Living* ones." Ebon flicked on his turn signal and went right at an intersection, still traveling west. In the side-view mirror, I noticed Mid was following us through the turn, signal blinking. "She might have a rough idea of where we are, but I can put up a screen of life that scrambles her senses and keeps her from pinpointing us." He chuckled. "Drives her crazy."

For the first time, I realized the cruiser was under shade, though the road and land ahead and behind were bathed in sunlight. Craning my neck, I leaned forward and looked up at the sky. A cloud of black insects hovered overhead, perfectly keeping pace with the cruiser.

"You're telling me she can't see us?" I asked, gaze fixed on the bugs above.

"As long as I keep my guard up," said Ebon. "Luckily, on guard is pretty much my permanent state of mind."

I settled back in the seat. I wasn't sure I believed him, but it was true we hadn't been attacked on the open road recently.

"So what's your deal, anyway?" I asked. "I don't remember you from when I was wired into the planet."

"No surprise there," said Ebon. "Didn't I just tell you I have a way of keeping out of sight?"

"Are you Landkind? A Groundswell Crossbreed? A Terralyzer? A deity of some kind?"

He laughed. "None of the above. What you see is what you get."

"Except for the controlling living things part."

He laughed again, harder. He annoyed me, but I couldn't bring myself to actively dislike him.

"That explains it," I said. "Why you're such a chick magnet. It's got nothing to do with your sex appeal, does it?" I smirked and shook my head. "You control *all* living things, including *people*."

Ebon looked at me sideways, grinning. "Sounds logical when you put it like that."

"So here's a question for you." I narrowed my eyes at him. "Are you controlling *me*, too?"

He chuckled. "Now that just wouldn't be respectful, would it? You being a former Mother Earth avatar and all."

"Hmm." I tapped my chin with my index finger. "Or maybe you *can't* influence an avatar, former or otherwise. Maybe that's why I haven't gone all googly over you like those other women."

"Possibly." He sounded thoughtful. "Or maybe I don't turn on the charm for someone I genuinely have feelings for. What do you think of that?"

"I'm a private detective, did you know that?" I said. "And I've run across a *lot* of con artists in my day, on the job. More *bullshitters* than you could shake a planet at."

"Is that what you think I am?" He clucked his tongue in dismay. "Have you gotten that jaded? Don't you believe in *anyone* or *anything* anymore?"

"Let me guess. You're just the guy to make me a believer again."

He looked at me then, intently. "What does it take?" When he asked the question, he seemed to be deeply serious, throwing off the lightness of our quippy interchange. "What does it take for Mother Earth herself to become so jaded?"

I felt uncomfortable and looked away. "Don't ask me. I'm the Earth's ex. Ask the new girl. The war-self or whatever. From what I've heard, she might say the *people* drove her to it."

"Have you ever felt that way, Gaia?" asked Ebon. "Whose side are you on?"

"Do you know what you get when you take the Earth Mother out of an avatar, Ebon?" I spread my arms dramatically. "You get *me*. You get a *human being*. So there's your answer, isn't it?"

"Maybe," said Ebon. "Or maybe you'd do just about anything to get back in Mommy's good graces."

"You want the truth?" I asked him.

"Sure, why not?"

"The truth is, my whole life has apparently been a lie, and the planet I was supposedly linked to did nothing to set me straight. Not to mention, she's in the process of trying to kill me as we speak." I took a deep breath and let it out slowly. "So, no, there isn't a whole lot of loyalty there right now."

Ebon cleared his throat. "Good to know," he said, and then we both fell silent and stayed that way as the road continued to unwind under the tires of the state police cruiser.

I have never been a child. That's one of the things about me.

My memory is sketchy about my vast past. I remember bits and pieces of multiple lives I've lived as an avatar of Mother Earth…but I have no memory at all of ever being an actual child. Always, I have joined my lives full-grown, awakening as a woman in her twenties with an adult's awareness of herself and the world around her.

And so, I have always felt cheated out of childhood. I have always thought I missed out on something special, and my lives have been the less because of it. I might have had the power to control dirt and stone, to channel the ley line energy of a world, and to sense and interact with primal and exotic physical forces in ways that are almost godlike, but I have never known the simple pleasures of being a little girl, seeing the world and everything in it from a child's point of view.

But I wondered, as Ebon drove onward, if I was getting a taste of it now.

Without my powers, I felt so much smaller. The scenery, as it fanned out around us, seemed so much bigger. Without any link to it, I felt less like a part of it and more like someone on the outside looking in, lacking true understanding…seeing the surface and nothing more.

Traveling as a passenger in someone else's car, giving over

control to another person, also made me think of how I imagined childhood must feel. I didn't even know where we were going or what exactly we would do when we got there. Could there have been anything more childlike than that?

Yet this was no fate I would have asked for myself. Maybe it would have been fun for a little kid who didn't know any better, but not so much for an adult, especially one who knew she was in mortal danger from a planet on the warpath. Running from a fight was never my style.

Nevertheless, I still forgot to feel like a grownup when we got to the Mississippi River at the western edge of Illinois.

Ebon let out a low whistle as we rolled onto Government Bridge at Rock Island. "What a river, huh?"

Watching from my open window, I couldn't look away from the giant expanse of river. It stretched as far as I could see into the distance, the afternoon sunlight dancing on its rippling brown waves. It swelled from bank to bank, girdling the land like a vast ribbon with a seemingly lazy flow that belied the true power of its raging current.

"It's something, all right," I told him.

How many times in how many lives had I crossed the Mississippi? How many times had I swum through it, or passed under it, in my travels?

And yet, this latest crossing felt like the first to me. The river dazzled me as if I'd never seen it before, as if I'd never experienced its beauty and grandeur in *any* of my lives.

It was as if I were a child, and the simple wonder of the moment overtook me. It was as if, for that brief time, wonder and joy were all that mattered.

"I can compliment you, can't I?" asked Ebon. "Like, 'nice job with the water feature,' right?"

I heard him, but I didn't answer. The smell of the river overwhelmed me, the smell of dirty water tinged with metal and fish. Something about it stirred distant memories, made me want to submerge.

"Let's just hope you-know-who doesn't catch us on the radar," said Ebon. "My blocking techniques don't always work so well around water. There's something about the reflectivity that cuts through my blurring ability."

I knew I should be worried, but I just kept looking out the window, fiddling with my braid as I admired the river. Far below, boats drifted in both directions, crossing paths mid-river. Canada geese swooped up from the water, even as a brown-winged hawk shot down to scoop up its fishy prey among the waves.

"Maybe you should try again to see if you can sense her," said Ebon. "Sense if the Earth's about to attack. Maybe you still have an echo of your connection."

I felt around with my mind for a moment, then shook my head. "I never knew this river could be so beautiful." Just as I said it, three gleaming fish leaped out of the water and splashed back down again.

We drove deep into Iowa that day, cutting across the state from Davenport to Des Moines and as far west as the state would take us. By the time we pulled in at the rundown old Star Brite Mo-Tel outside of Sioux City, it was long past sundown—half past eleven o'clock.

At which point I was totally dead on my feet. I hadn't slept much in the car; I'd been too captivated by the scenery of the wide-open Midwestern plains.

"It's just a bunch of cornfields," Ebon had said.

"I know." The novelty of seeing the world without being plugged into it still hadn't worn off for me. "Cool, huh?"

But as soon as Mid got the key to our shared room, I wanted only to pass out on my bed. It had been a very long day, to say the least.

Unfortunately, she kept running her mouth to Ebon and me in the parking lot. "I'm not picking up anything to suggest an attack is imminent." She raised her hands in front of her, closed her eyes, and turned in a slow circle. "But as we know, I'm not as sensitive as I once was."

"Seems like a safe location to me," said Ebon. "As safe as they come, anyway. There's an old Superfund hazardous waste cleanup site within a half-mile of this place. That'll put out plenty of static, and I'm adding to the interference."

Mid nodded. "First sign of trouble, raise the alarm, and we run."

"Fight and run, you mean," said Ebon.

"Sure, why the hell not?" Mid shrugged. "Then we get an early start and hit the road again. We've got a few more hours to get where we're going."

"Which is?" I asked through a yawn…the latest of many.

"South Dakota." Mid pointed away from the motel, into the darkness. "Thataway."

"Could you be more specific?" I said.

Ebon nodded. "Have you ever been to Mount Rushmore?"

"Kind of," I told him. "My energy form passed through it along a ley line conduit once or twice."

"Doesn't count," said Mid.

"And you won't get there this time, either, sorry to say." Ebon smirked and socked my upper arm. "Because that is *not* where we're going."

"Then *where*? Just *tell* me."

"Figure it out," said Ebon. "There aren't that many notable sites in South Dakota, after all."

With a chuckle, he marched past me and headed for his room, which was right next door to ours. He spun the motel key ring on an index finger as he walked, then jammed the key into the front door lock and gave it a twist. On his way inside, he gave us a jaunty wave.

"Whatever." I reached out toward Mid, feeling ready to pass out. "Give me the key. I'm exhausted."

"Hold on," said Mid. "There's something we need to talk about first."

"Tell me in the morning." I couldn't remember ever being so tired in my life. Maybe being an avatar had given me a tolerance to lack of sleep that normal folks didn't have. Now that the avatar aspect was gone, I craved rest like a natural-born human.

I turned to shuffle toward the room…and the parking lot surface pushed up in front of me, thrusting a ridge of jagged asphalt in my path.

Looking back, I saw Mid with both hands outstretched, shaking. A pulsing golden light surrounded her, flashing with sparks like little moths off a bug zapper.

I almost laughed, almost asked if the low ridge of asphalt was the best she could do…but I didn't. At least she had *some* power left, which was more than *I* could say.

"Gaia." She walked over to me. "How easy do you think it is to lie to Mother Earth or her avatar?"

I shrugged. "Pretty damn easy, apparently. I've been lied to all my life."

Mid shook her head. "Imagine keeping secrets from an entire *planet*. From the very world you live on. It would take *vast* power, wouldn't it?"

"Maybe." I frowned, wondering what she was getting at.

"It would take a *conspiracy*," said Mid. "And such a thing would not be easily exposed, would it? Especially when the *actual* planet has disengaged from her avatar and is on a serious warpath against anyone who disagrees with her mission."

"Sounds about right," I said. "Now, why are you telling me this?"

"Tomorrow, we are going to see someone and ask for their help," explained Mid. "From her point of view, we might represent great danger. I expect her to react as if she's under attack. I expect her to fight as if her life depends on it."

"I still don't…"

"And *none* of us is necessarily ready for that fight," said Mid. "You need to know that going in. You need to prepare for the worst."

"How can I *prepare* if I don't even know what we're trying to *accomplish?*"

"By reaching deep inside and finding the part of you that is capable," said Mid. "Capable of *anything,* if that's what it takes."

I shook my head. "That part doesn't exist. I'm not who you think I am."

She stepped forward and jabbed me in the chest with one bony finger. "It's *exactly* who you are. If you look *hard* enough, you'll *see* it."

I couldn't stop the next yawn from coming. "May I *please* just go to bed? I can barely…"

Without warning, she grabbed the front of my leather jacket and yanked me down to face her. "Your *twin* was not the *only* war-self to walk the Earth."

Then, she gave me one last shake, let go of my jacket, and stomped off toward the room. I followed, my mind starting to churn in spite of my utter physical exhaustion.

I fell asleep as soon as my head hit the pillow, but it was still a restless night for me. I slipped in and out of awareness, fully formed thoughts jumping into my head, then popping like soap bubbles as I slipped under again.

Sometimes, I drifted into dreams in which I was very present, interacting with my friends back home in Confluence. I dreamt of Duke and Luna and Nephelae and Ashanti, all living together in my office. I dreamt of making love to Sheriff Briar, sometimes on a beach by the ocean, though we had never been there together before.

Then, there were the strange and distant dreams I barely remember, the ones full of faces and things I couldn't identify. They must have come from past lives, I thought, handed down from one avatar to the next, devoid now of any recognizable form or context. In some of them, there weren't even people or anything I'd think of as life or its common interactions; they left me with weird feelings that lingered long after I rose from the arcane, abstract depths.

Once, those unknown depths even left me with no memory of who *I* was. Floating up out of them, I opened my eyes, staring at the ceiling—and completely forgot everything about myself. I lay there, blank as a fresh diary, unable even to come up with my name... utterly terrified at the emptiness.

It was as if I'd been somehow reset or restored to factory settings, wiping out everything I knew. All my joys were gone, all the moments that had made up the life I'd lived...and all the worries, too.

What if it were permanent? What if I *never* regained my memory and had to go through life like that, a complete cypher, starting over?

The truth was, though, that part of me welcomed it. Part of me was glad for the forgiveness that came with forgetting and for the shirking of whatever responsibilities had troubled me before everything went blank.

But then, it all came back in one huge, onrushing wave. Suddenly and without explanation, I knew who I was again, and where I'd come from, and what had happened. All the fearful possibilities of tomorrow crashed in upon me, and the weight of what I'd been told was my burden to bear.

The burden of saving humanity from being wiped out, though I had no idea how that was remotely possible without my powers and team of supporters back home.

So much for a good night's sleep.

13

The morning was scorching as we drove up into South Dakota. Though heat like that had never bothered me before, when my powers and planetary link were running fine, it kicked my ass now. It was especially bad any time we stopped, and the wind ceased to flow through the cruiser's windows. Those were the times when I'd just sweat under the blazing sun, wishing for a cool body of water to jump into.

I also wished that Ebon would just switch on the damn air conditioning in the car. Unlike me, he had a high tolerance for heat and preferred it to lower temperatures. Not to mention, he claimed the A/C negatively impacted his car's performance and fuel economy. He actually had it disabled, so just switching it on wasn't even an option.

It was things like that that made me wish I could have my powers back, even if it was just for a moment…just long enough to knock some earthly sense into him.

"I finally figured out what you are," I told him. "What your super-power is."

"Tell me," he said. "This oughtta be good."

"You're a colossal pain in the ass," I told him. "In *my* ass."

"I won't deny it." Ebon chuckled. "But that's not the *only* thing that's special about me."

By the time we got to Badlands National Park, five and a half hours out from Sioux City, I didn't care if I never saw that cruiser, or its driver, again. Looking back, I saw the Corolla behind us with the windows rolled up—presumably, because the A/C was running. Mid looked perfectly cool at the wheel, even giving me a little wave of acknowledgement. For the umpteenth time, I wished I'd ridden with her that morning.

But I'd liked Ebon so much at first. How could I have misjudged him so badly?

"This is it," he said after paying the park fee to the ranger at the gate and rolling through to wait for Mid. "First stop, the Badlands."

Looking around at the dry, dusty ground and low scrub, I tried to remember if I'd been there before. The place seemed familiar… but no, it didn't ring any bells. It was still possible I'd passed through as an immaterial form on my way to somewhere else, but I couldn't be sure and maybe never would.

"This is one of my favorite places in the world," said Ebon as Mid caught up and we started rolling again. "You thought you saw some scenic sights yesterday? Today will totally blow your mind."

"Cool." I was too busy thinking about what Mid had said was in store for us in the Badlands to say more than that. Whoever awaited and whatever they'd do, my fear meter was cranked up to eleven. Mid had set out last night to get me worried…and she'd accomplished her mission with ease.

"So, where exactly are we going?" I asked. "Do you even know?"

Just then, Ebon pulled to one side, and Mid zipped past, taking the lead position in our convoy.

"There's your answer," he said. "The one with the best radar will get us where we need to go."

As we continued in her wake, the park opened up before us… and I was awestruck. Whatever experience I might have had passing through there in a noncorporeal form before, it could not have prepared me for the experience of seeing the place in person.

Like the skyline of a city, an array of rugged peaks and spires spanned the horizon under sapphire skies. In the bright morning sunlight, distinct layers of different colored rock were visible, bands of gray, rust, and brown stretching through the magnificent sprawl.

On the way to that skyline, humps and ridges of banded rock

straddled the green plain, islands of gray and red and yellow afloat as if upon a calm, flat sea. In either direction along the rough-cut shield wall ahead, those ridges, rises, and buttes marched off into the distance, a seemingly endless atoll cresting the world.

When we followed the road further, it carried us into the towering skyline, filtering us between foothills and outcroppings with the same layered structure. Domes and declivities appeared along the road—then kingdoms of fairy-tale steeples and minarets that looked as if they'd been dripped out of candle wax.

We finally pulled off in the shelter of a stone canopy, its pale gray shell shaped by the wind in a smooth bowl. It was open at both ends for the passage of vehicles, and three windows were cut in the stone at scattered points—only one of them near the ground, and that fifteen feet up along the bell of the canopy.

I was breathless as I got out of the cruiser and looked around, taking in the natural wonder that sheltered us. Once again, cut off from my link with the Earth, I felt more overwhelmed than ever by the staggering beauty around me—more like a child enraptured by what to her is fathomless, magical grandeur, not just the product of natural elements and physical forces.

"Stay close," said Ebon as he got out of the car. "We don't know for sure how this will go."

"Sure we do." Mid approached us from the Corolla. "My money's on it being a total cluster…"

A loud rumbling under the canopy cut her off. The three of us stood together, looking around, as the ground shook under our feet.

The quake intensified fast, nearly knocking me over…but Ebon caught my arm and kept me upright. His gaze met mine briefly, and I thought I glimpsed genuine concern in those warm, dark eyes.

As for Mid, she seemed the steadiest of us all, completely unfazed. She closed her eyes and spread her arms wide, speaking loud enough to be heard over the rumbling. "Lady of the Badlands, hear us. We come only in peace to discuss matters of great import."

As if in reply, the ground shook harder. A spike of gray-and-rust banded stone thrust out of the sand not three yards away from where Mid was standing.

Still, she seemed unbothered. "White Buffalo Calf Woman, we humbly ask your forgiveness for disrupting the wilderness of your domain with our concerns. If there were any other way, we would not have interrupted your blessed slumber."

Another spike punched up from the ground nearby, then another. I heard a cracking sound overhead and looked up in time to see a spike extrude and snap off from the canopy, plunging downward. It missed us all by a few yards, but the message was clear.

The Lady of the Badlands could kill us at any moment.

Heart pounding, I was seized by the impulse to jump in the car or just run as far as I could. It's funny how, when you don't have powers, you soon start to think like an average human being.

But I fought back the urge and stood my ground alongside Ebon and Mid. It wasn't like the Lady's reaction was a surprise, after all; Mid had warned me the night before that things could go like this.

Maybe Ebon saw the stirrings of panic in my eyes, because he dropped a hand on my shoulder. "We'll be fine." His voice didn't sound as reassuring as perhaps he'd intended. "And it could be worse. At least Big Mama Earth isn't the one bringing down the hammer."

As he said it, more rocky spikes shot out of the ground, surrounding us. Their points were aimed right at us; I could imagine what kind of damage they'd do if they shot up close enough to catch our soft parts.

Meanwhile, Mid's voice grew louder. "Please, Lady! We ask for an audience, not a fight! The matter we want to discuss is of grave importance to us all…and all of humanity, as well!"

Cracks opened in the ground, widening as they ripped toward us. Dust and fragments rained down from the canopy, followed by showers of dartlike spikes. Holes blew open, ejecting hunks of rock like cannonballs that blasted the Corolla, smashing the windows and pummeling the car's metal body as if it were tinfoil.

The skeletal bison came next, wrenching up from the ground one after another. There were three, then five, then seven, all enormous, at least twice the size of any bison or buffalo I'd ever seen. They tossed their great horned heads with restless vehemence and pawed the earth with their hooves, backs arched.

More rose up with each passing minute, clambering out of ancient, dusty tombs. When they got around to charging, I couldn't see how we could possibly survive that monstrous rank.

Another volley of cannonball rocks pounded the Corolla, obliterating every glass surface and leaving the doors, roof, and hoods a crumpled wreck. Again, spikes surged out of the ground, and debris showered down from above.

Two bison launched themselves across the ruined ground, horns forward, aiming right at the little old lady calling out to their mistress.

"Stop!" Mid swung her arms around, aiming at the charging bison, and glared with dark intensity. Golden light pulsed around her hands, then shot out of them in twin, blazing beams.

One of the beams blew apart a bison in mid-run, flinging the white shrapnel of its shattered bones in all directions. But the second beam missed its target.

It was then that Ebon stepped forward and raised his arms overhead. A strange black nimbus swirled around him, so his body looked like a negative exposure, etched in white against the darkness. He chanted something in a language I didn't understand, and bolts of blackness flashed out of him.

All the bison stampeded at once, roaring in the sweltering heat. The bolts slashed through them in quick succession, changing their bleached white bones into gouts of black smoke that puffed up and whirled away.

"I end you *again!*" he cried. "I banish your breed from the face of the Earth for now and evermore!"

The rumbling and blasts faded for an instant, but it didn't last. The noise and shaking and eruptions surged again, more powerful than before.

This time, they were joined by crackling arcs of ley line energy snapping out of the ground. They clustered around Mid, lashing at her from all sides with searing energy. She deflected them as best she could, but one got through, leaving a sizzling line like a lit fuse between her shoulder blades.

That was when I realized we were doomed. The Bitch of the Badlands was going to kill us.

Unless someone tried something unexpected.

I thought it through for an instant, digging deep…and then I burst into action. Darting from Ebon's side, I ducked inside the cruiser and hit the horn.

"Hey!" I held the horn down and hollered over its blare. "Badlands Woman! Listen up!"

The energy bolts and rumbling didn't let up.

"I said *hey!*" I shouted louder and pounded the horn on and off, changing the steady blare to staccato blasts. "Don't you *recognize* me?"

Only then, at last, did the attack subside.

About time. Laying off the cruiser's horn, I ran over to the demolished Corolla and clambered up onto its battered roof. "You *do*, don't you? You *recognize* the number one war-self of planet Earth!" I paused. "Or should I say, you *think* you do."

I waited just long enough for my words to sink in.

"Here's the thing," I said. "If I was who you *think* I am, wouldn't I have already kicked your *ass*? And wouldn't a certain *planet* be backing me up, tearing you a new one?"

There was no reply…but the rumbling didn't start up again, so I thought maybe I was doing okay.

"What if, instead of *her*, I'm someone who just *looks* like her? What if my friends and I are on *your* side, and we're only here to talk?"

I stopped talking then and waited for whatever came next. Would another herd of skeletal bison charge out of the earth to gore and trample us? Would more cannonball rocks burst out of the ground and smash us flat? Would the entire rock canopy crash in and entomb us?

When a fresh round of rumbling started, I thought I'd failed. I looked over at Ebon, and he just shrugged, as if to say, *c'est la vie.*

A mound of banded stone broke through the ground then, pushing up into the middle of the flat under the canopy. It rose to a height of several feet, then stopped, sand running off all its sides like water.

The mound just sat there for a moment, inscrutable, and I wondered if I should move closer. When I finally took a step toward it, though, it started to shake, and I stopped.

As I watched, transfixed, the top of the mound blew right off, shooting shrapnel all around. Instinctively, I threw an arm up and closed my eyes to shield myself.

When I opened them, I saw a shimmering figure clad in white

rise up from the mound, an ethereal woman with red-tinted skin and long, black hair. She wore a snow white dress with a thick fur collar and trim, studded from shoulder to ankle with glittering teardrop diadems.

Slender and sinuous, she floated above the mound in a state of perfect grace. Her eyes, when she turned them to me, were equal parts serene and indignant.

"I am the White Buffalo Calf Woman." When she spoke, her voice sounded like the rush of wind over the prairie. "I am the Lady of the Badlands, the goddess of the Lakota Sioux. If you are not the Risen Shadow, the One Who Destroys, then who are you and what do you want?"

As in the dark as I was about the specifics of our quest, there were only one detail I was sure of just then. "I want to save humankind."

White Buffalo gazed at me for a moment, searching. "That is not what the Earth and her war-self desire. You would stand against them in this?"

"Yes, Lady," I said. "What good is a world without its people?"

She continued to stare thoughtfully at me. "Yet you are cut from the same cloth as the world's war-self. You were made to be identical in every way. Why should I trust what you say?"

"Because I am *not* her," I said. "And I will not *rest* until I have taken back my good name and mantle, which she has *ruined.*"

Suddenly, White Buffalo swept forward, coming to rest directly in front of me. Hair rippling like swaying palm fronds, eyes glowing with sharp white light, she fixed me in her gaze. I felt like a butterfly pinned to a board, under the lens of a powerful microscope.

"And why have you come here, little warrior?" she asked. "What do you want from *me?*"

Mid spoke for me. "Help," she said. "We want your help to save humanity before it's too late."

"But I am not *strong* enough to challenge Mother Earth or her minions," said White Buffalo.

"Perhaps not alone," said Mid. "But that is not what we seek. We ask that you help restore the Ancestrum and empower the rightful war-self for this era."

"Her, you mean." White Buffalo's gaze never wavered from my face. "This one."

Heart pounding, I waited for the answer. When Mid had told me my twin was not the only war-self to have walked the Earth, it hadn't occurred to me that *I* might be the other. Maybe I should have guessed, but I hadn't.

And now the truth was on the tip of Mid's tongue, and the implications were staggering. *Overwhelming.*

"Yes," said Mid. "Her. The woman who calls herself Gaia Charmer."

A chill rose up my spine as I heard the words. So many thoughts were flashing through my mind, so many questions were fighting to burst out—yet I somehow stayed silent, holding back as the Lady of the Badlands considered her options.

As little as I yet knew, I was well aware that humanity's future depended on her answer.

"You came here uninvited," she said at last. "And one of you came in the form of a terrible adversary. I am well within my rights as an ancient patroness of these lands to *wipe* you all away as if you never existed."

I tensed, wondering if my death was imminent. Now that I finally knew a kernel of the truth about myself, was I about to be blown out of existence by a Native American goddess?

"Perhaps we would all be better off that way," said White Buffalo. "Humanity has not done much for me lately. The people do seem to be locked on the road to self-destruction, with no inclination to seek a different path.

"And yet..." White Buffalo reached toward me. When her hand touched my cheek, a flicker of electricity passed through me. "I cannot deny that I am moved by your pleas. And as much as I wish I could set aside my affections for feckless humankind, I cannot do that, either. *Yet.*"

Withdrawing her hand, she drifted away. When she waved, the rocky spikes withdrew into the ground, and the cannonballs of stone dissolved into sand. The holes in the earth filled, and every trace of bison bone turned to dust and swirled away.

"So be it," she said. "I will do what is within my power to do, in the name of humanity."

"Thank you, milady," said Mid.

"Be advised, though," said White Buffalo. "This work you ask might well remain beyond our grasp. Restoring the Ancestrum will be no simple task and will take us far afield. As for empowering the rightful war-self, I'm not even sure it can be done."

"I can tell you this," said Mid. "On our own, without your help, we stand almost *zero* chance of success. So we'll be more than willing to cast our lot with you."

"Better than nothing?" White Buffalo smiled as she drifted down to land her pale feet on the ground. "I am honored you place me in such very high esteem."

"Your esteem couldn't be higher," I said, jumping down from the crushed roof of the car. Marching up to her, I extended my hand. "If we manage to pull this off because of you, you'll be known forever as the savior of humanity."

She cocked her head and gazed at me for a moment as if taking my measure. "It has a nice ring to it." With a nod, she took my hand and shook it. "Congratulations. You have done the near-impossible. You have won *me* to your cause."

My hand tingled with more of the same charge I got any time she touched me. "I'm glad to hear it, Lady Buffalo. Now, maybe *you* can tell me." I squeezed her hand and looked over at Mid and Ebon, who didn't seem the slightest bit agitated. "Where do we go next, anyway?"

"Vancouver, far to the north and west of here," said White Buffalo. "The gateway to somewhere you have never been, which is where our only hope of survival lies."

I frowned. "*You* don't know me. How do you know I haven't been there?"

"Because *no one* alive in the outside world at this time ever has been." White Buffalo looked grave as she said it.

"Really?" My frown deepened. "You *know* I was the avatar of Mother Earth, right? I know this planet like the back of my hand."

White Buffalo smiled cryptically. "There are secrets even Mother Earth and her vessels don't know about this planet…thank the Great Spirit for that."

With that, she let go of my hand and turned to face Mid, who had come up behind her.

"We might already be too late," said White Buffalo. "You know that, don't you?"

"We'll move forward as if we have even the slightest chance of success," said Mid. "Otherwise, we'd be declaring surrender."

"All right then." White Buffalo nodded. "Courage it is." She wove her hands through the air, and a cloud of mist surrounded her. When it cleared, her long, white gown had been replaced by a scoop-neck white top and faded bluejeans. "Shall we begin? Let's not keep the world waiting."

14

Why stay the night in Yellowstone National Park when there's a perfectly good toxic lake just a few hours northwest of the place?

That was the thinking, anyway, as we skipped one of the most beautiful places on Earth and headed for one of the most contaminated—the Berkeley Pit, old open-pit mine in Butte, Montana. Since Mother Earth couldn't see as well through pollution, we guessed this place would keep us well-hidden overnight, even if we stayed at a motel a few miles down the road.

I hoped the theory was sound, because I was in no shape for an all-out battle after the fight with White Buffalo Calf Woman and nine hours in a now-crowded state police cruiser racing away from the Badlands. With the Corolla demolished and an extra passenger along for the ride, we now had four people in the cruiser—Ebon, Mid, White Buffalo, and me. It wasn't really cramped, but there wasn't as much room to stretch out as before, and there was a bit too much body heat in the A/C-free cabin. With the Midwestern heat wave in full swing, the temperature inside the car was pegging big-time in the sweltering zone.

Not that it seemed to bother White Buffalo a bit. She sat up front with Ebon, looking cool and collected at all times, as Mid and I squirmed and sweated in the back seat. Something in her goddess

DNA must have given her resistance to the heat…though it didn't protect her from every environmental influence, as we discovered.

The closer we got to Butte and the Berkeley Pit, the more uncomfortable White Buffalo got. She slumped in her seat, rubbing her temples, and drained of color.

When she started groaning, Ebon took notice. "What's wrong?" he asked. "Are you all right?"

White Buffalo just tossed her head and groaned some more. Then, suddenly, she lashed an arm across the seat and grabbed his wrist.

"Stop!"

Instantly, Ebon swung the cruiser to the side of the road. Before it had even stopped moving, White Buffalo flung the door open and scrambled out, falling to her knees.

I'd never seen a goddess throw up before. For the next few moments, White Buffalo looked all too human, retching repeatedly on the gravel berm.

Jumping out after her, I stayed close and waited for her to finish. When she finally stopped, I put a hand on her back.

"Feel better?" I understood her pain. When my link to Mother Earth was active, extreme pollution made me feel the same way.

She nodded weakly, and I helped her to her feet. "This place is making me sick. It's so full of *poison.*"

"We'll pass the actual Berkeley Pit soon," said Ebon from behind the wheel. "Hopefully, the effects will let up when we get on the other side of it."

"I hope you're right," said White Buffalo. "I can't take much more of this."

We got back in the cruiser then and drove onward. White Buffalo got sicker and had to get out again a mile down the road— but the effects started to lessen after we passed the turnoff for the Berkeley Pit.

Unfortunately, they were still pretty potent when we reached the first motel after the turnoff, three miles away. White Buffalo made it clear she couldn't spend the night there, so we drove another three miles to a motel she could manage. Waves of pain were still battering her, but she thought she could make do until morning.

She got her own room and disappeared inside. After more than nine hours on the road, the rest of us were happy to do the same.

Again, I shared a room with Mid, who looked almost as beat as White Buffalo. She turned up the air conditioner in the window, then lay down on her bed beside it right away with a heavy sigh.

"Are you okay, Mid?" I asked as I got my own bed ready.

She spoke without opening her eyes. "I've been getting the same feedback as White Buffalo Calf Woman...not as bad, but bad enough to give me a splitting headache."

"Would a cool washcloth help?"

"No, thank you."

I glanced at her satchel on the dresser in front of the beds. "Do you have any ibuprofen or aspirin in there?"

"Just...no." She tossed her head from side to side. "I just want to lie here quietly for a while." She sounded annoyed. "With the lights off."

"All right." I walked over to the switch on the wall by the door and flicked it off...then heard something tapping on the window. Peering out from behind the floral-print drape, I saw Ebon standing just outside, waving.

Whatever he wanted, I thought getting out of the room for a while was a good idea. I had a hunch Mid would be happy about it.

"I'm going to see what Ebon wants," I said. "I'll be back in a bit." Then, I scooped up the room key from atop the TV set, dropped it in my pocket, and let myself out.

Mid just lay there with her head cradled in her hands and didn't say a word.

As I closed the door softly behind me, Ebon gestured at the room. "She's asleep already?"

I shook my head. "She's got a bad headache from the pollution."

"Sorry to hear that." He nodded toward the cruiser. "Want to come along? I have an errand to run."

"If you're sure Mid and Buffalo will be okay," I said.

"They should be fine." Ebon headed for the car. "We won't be gone long."

Standing behind a chain link fence atop a steep green-and-yellow bank, I gazed down at the dark red water far below. The color shifted as I watched, red giving way to deep green blooms as a faint breeze played across the surface.

The sun, which was low in the sky, cast a shadow from the rim that covered at least half of the immense, teardrop-shaped lake. In a matter of minutes, the sun would set, and the pit's transformation for the night would be complete.

"Hard to believe something so polluted can be so beautiful, huh?" said Ebon, who'd driven us out here and paid our admission fees.

I just nodded and kept staring into the shifting colors of the water.

"That's humanity for you." Ebon elbowed me and laughed. "Gotta love 'em, those dirty dogs."

I wasn't as entertained as he was, though it was interesting getting so close to a thing like the Berkeley Pit. If I'd still had my link to the Earth, I probably would have dropped to the ground long ago, gasping for breath.

"You still haven't told me," I said. "Why did we need to come out here?"

"Part of my job." He leaned over the fence and stared into the water with narrowed eyes. "If a call comes in, and I'm nearby, I answer it."

"What kind of call?" I asked. "What are you talking about?"

"There." He pointed at the water, but all I saw were fluffy white clouds and blue sky reflected from overhead. "See that fish over there?"

Still, I didn't see what he was talking about. "What fish?"

"A new species," said Ebon. "It came into being a month ago, evolved to thrive on the toxic chemicals and heavy metals in the Pit. Sadly, its kind won't last." As he said it, a strip of silver wriggled up to the surface. "The end is nigh."

"I didn't think *anything* could live in there, except some extreme microbes," I said. "According to the plaques, anyway." I pointed to the long wooden panels mounted outside the visitor center, where the hazardous environment of the Pit was explained in detail.

"Well, *that* little fella could…at least for a while. If scientists had found and studied him, he might even have helped humanity survive climate change in the future…but, alas, he stayed under the radar." Ebon snapped his fingers, and the wriggling fish fell still. "May he and his species forever rest in peace."

I stared for a moment as the dead fish drifted on the blood red water. "So how did you know about him? What did you mean when you said a call came in?"

"As I said, it's my job. It's who I am. I'm in tune with all the species on the planet." He held out a hand, and the little fish floated up out of the water and came to rest in his palm. Its scales were silver, streaked with red and green like the water in the pit. "When a species is about to die out, I'm drawn to it. I capture its potential…" The fish suddenly flopped around in his hand, glowing—then stopped. "…and then I usher its kind from the world, never to be seen again."

"I see." As I watched, the fish turned into a mist and blew away. "You're some kind of…avatar of extinction?"

"Close enough." He smiled. "I do think of myself as an extinctionist, though that's probably too narrow a term for what I am. As you know, I can also control forms of life, make them do my bidding…though that's as much a function of my core nature as anything. Since I am the force at the end of all species' existence, life is drawn to me like a moth to a flame. Living things obey me because they instinctively recognize me as their master."

I nodded slowly, taking in what he was telling me. The sun, meanwhile, dropped to meet the horizon. The clouds arrayed around it turned redder than the water in the pit, which took on an orange hue. The blue sky flamed yellow, brighter than molten metal in a foundry.

"Sounds like you're pretty important in the scheme of things," I said. "Sounds like I ought to remember you from my days of being one with the planet."

He shrugged. "Like I told you before, I have a way of confusing Mother Earth. It doesn't surprise me that you never knew I was there."

I wasn't sure that made sense, but I let it ride for now. "So why did you bring me with you this evening? You didn't need me to finish your errand, obviously."

"This might be my job, but it gets lonely sometimes." He turned to me, smiling. "I wanted some company, and it just so happens I enjoy yours."

My guard went up at the tone of his voice. I wasn't sure, but it seemed like he might have something else in—

Without warning, he leaned over and kissed me on the lips.

It was a quick kiss, just a peck, but the message was clear. Things had just gotten complicated between us.

"Like I said." He leaned back, eyes wide, watching my face. "I enjoy your company."

He looked handsome by the burning light of the fading sunset, tinted with red and gold…but I couldn't let this go further. I'd been with Dale for a while, and staying true to him was important.

So why didn't I just tell him right then that I already had a boyfriend?

"Look, I…" Instead, I fumbled around and left the damn door open. "We should get back to the motel, shouldn't we? Check on Mid and White Buffalo?"

Ebon smiled and nodded. "Sure, that's what we should do. We're done here for now, anyway."

"Right," I said, and we walked away from the pit. On the way back to the cruiser, we didn't talk…though my mind was working overtime.

I couldn't help wondering why that kiss, as brief as it had been, had seemed so different. Did it have to do with his supernatural nature? Was I just another moth drawn to a flame, no matter how self-destructive it might be?

Did it have to do with my being disconnected from the spirit of the Earth, forced to focus more intently on the intricacies of my own human senses? Or did it have to do with something else altogether, something I didn't want to consider?

Had my feelings for Dale Briar changed? Did I unwittingly leave my love for him behind when I escaped his cell in Confluence?

15

We started early and drove all day the next day, heading west. Our route took us through vast stretches of national forest and reservation lands, sprawling from Montana into Washington state. When we crossed the Indian reservations, I looked for a reaction from White Buffalo, who was sitting up front—but she just stared and said nothing, stone-faced. Whatever her feelings might have been, she wasn't sharing them.

We passed Spokane, then hooked north at Seattle on I-5, heading for our destination. Rain dogged us all the way to the Canadian border, making the roads gleam with a mirror sheen of water.

None of us said much on the drive that day. A few times, I tried to get information out of Mid and Ebon, but they just deflected my questions with small talk. Most of the time, Mid had her eyes closed anyway, though I had my doubts that she was always asleep.

At least White Buffalo tried to make a little conversation here and there, seemingly taking an interest in me. She asked me where I lived, what I liked to do, and if I had a boyfriend or husband. I didn't say much about that particular subject, and Ebon made it a point to turn his attention elsewhere.

It was late in the day when we finally reached the border with Canada. I was nervous of course, considering I was a fugitive murder suspect, but Mid and Ebon assured me everything would be fine.

"But we're in an Indiana State Police vehicle," I said, worrying as we approached the checkpoint. "Won't that look suspicious, crossing the border from Washington state?"

"Gaia, I've got this." Ebon flashed a smile over his shoulder. "Trust me."

I folded my arms over my chest and slumped in my seat. I felt so vulnerable and exposed without my powers, even riding in a state police cruiser with three supernatural beings.

My heart hammered as our car got in line. If things went wrong, what would we do? Fight our way out of the checkpoint and make a run for it? Surrender to the authorities?

Too soon, we were next in line at the checkpoint booth. Again, Ebon flashed me a smile. "Relax."

Mid even opened her eyes and reached over to give my arm a squeeze. "We'll be fine, honey. *This* isn't the part I'm worried about."

When we drew up to the window, the agent in the booth—a young, blonde woman in a dark blue uniform and black bulletproof vest—smiled and asked to see Ebon's license. He reached over, empty-handed, and she reached down as if lifting a license from his palm. Then, she raised her hand as if to examine the nonexistent license…and returned it to him with a smile.

A few questions later, and she waved us through. Ebon had gotten us over the border as promised, with no fuss.

"What'd I tell you?" He laughed as we drove away from the checkpoint. "Nothing to worry about."

I did feel relieved and smiled when he looked back in the rearview mirror…though I couldn't deny the scene had given me the creeps anyway. His power to control living things came in pretty handy—but how could I ever be sure he wasn't using it on me?

And if he did, would I even know it?

We checked in at an upscale hotel in downtown Vancouver, British Columbia, courtesy of Ebon's powers of persuasion, then went to eat at a nearby dim sum place. White Buffalo had no idea what dim sum was, but she agreed to at least see what it looked like.

"So, what's this next place we're going?" I asked her. "The one you said Vancouver's a gateway to?"

"You'll see," she said, her eyes taking in the hustle and bustle around us. "Tomorrow."

"Well, you have my curiosity piqued. You said no one alive has ever been there, and it's hidden even from Mother Earth herself."

"I don't want to spoil it for you," said White Buffalo. "It's better if you experience it firsthand without any preconceptions."

"Could someone at least tell me why we're going there?" I was fed up with the secrecy. "What does this place have to do with stopping the war twin and saving humanity?"

"Hold on." Mid fluttered a hand in the air. "Is that our waiter?" She did it again, half getting up from the table.

"Enough!" I smacked the table with my palm, making the glasses and silverware rattle. Suddenly, everyone at the table (and beyond) was paying attention. "Somebody tell me *something*."

"All right." Mid saw people at other tables staring and settled back down into her seat. "You already know our mission, Gaia. We're going to try to restore the Ancestrum and empower the true war-self for this era. You also know that *you* are the true war-self."

"This Ancestrum," I said. "Who are they?"

"They're like us," said Mid. "Like *me*, is more like it. They are past avatars of the Earth, retired from active service—hidden away, forgotten. But they still have *power*, and that's what we need right now."

I frowned. "Not enough power to take on the planet, surely."

Mid shrugged. "We won't know until we try."

Ebon cleared his throat then. "Can we please order our dim sum and deal with this later?"

"I have another question first," I said, smacking the table with the laminated menu. "Why are there two war selves?"

"Why not?" said Ebon.

"Seriously," I continued. "If a war-self is so powerful, why does the Earth need *two* of them?"

"It doesn't matter," said Mid. "All you need to know is that there *are* two, and you're one of them."

"But *why?*" I knew people around us were looking when I smacked the menu down again, but I didn't care. "Did she whip up a second one because I wasn't tough enough on polluters? Because I didn't stop climate change single-handedly?"

Mid looked more uncomfortable than ever. "I said, it doesn't matter."

"It matters to me!" I snapped. "I need to know the full story before I take on the damn *planet.*"

Mid rubbed her forehead and mumbled something I couldn't make out.

"What was that?" I leaned forward. "What did you just say?"

"All right," hissed Ebon, glaring at the both of us. "That's enough! Save the nastiness for the battle ahead."

"It might not be much of a *battle* if I don't know what I'm *in* for," I told him.

"Okay, okay." Ebon threw up his hands in surrender. "Let's just get through dinner, and then I'll take you somewhere and give you answers. Can you be just a little more patient?"

"I'm done being patient!" I said. "I've gone along with you people like a good little captive, and I'm damn *sick* of it."

"I'm starved," he said, watching as the waiter glanced at our table, then passed us by yet again. "Just let me get some dim sum, and I promise you'll get answers for dessert. Deal?"

I still wasn't happy, but I did settle back in my chair. "Okay then. Deal."

We shook on it. Then, Ebon caught the waiter and proceeded to order steamed pork buns and more. He ordered one of everything on the menu, in fact, and the square table quickly filled up with a dim sum feast for four.

I ate morsels of the Chinese food put in front of me, but my mind was elsewhere. All I could think about was getting the answers I'd been promised, wherever the hell that might take me.

The sun had gone down, and the sky had turned shades of rose and violet. Lights sparkled from the cityscape below and carpeted the hillsides surrounding the bay. All of it lay at our feet, fanning out in a glittering panorama from the windows of our lofty perch.

That was where Ebon had taken me after dinner, to a downtown tower called the Vancouver Lookout. It was the perfect place to see the city, he'd said, especially at night.

"Beautiful view, isn't it?" Ebon gazed out at the harbor, where glowing boats skimmed the water, their lights reflected in bright streaks over the smooth surface. "So peaceful and soothing from all the way up here. A real vision of the harmony that's possible between humanity and the natural world."

My mind was on other topics, but I nodded in agreement anyway. I hadn't cared where we went, as long as he gave me the answers I wanted, so I'd gone along with it. But now that we were here, it felt more like a date than a revelation…a date with a third wheel along for the ride, that is.

"Humanity is not *entirely* without talent," said White Buffalo from a nearby window. I was glad she'd invited herself along when she'd heard where we were going, though Mid had gone back to the hotel instead. Having someone else with us took some of the pressure off me in case Ebon decided to make some kind of move.

"This shows you what the human race can do on the positive side," he said. "This is the work of humankind at their best. If anyone ever wonders why the human race should not be destroyed, send them up here."

He was right about the beauty of the view. Against my better judgment, I even got caught up in it a little; again, it seemed I appreciated scenery all the more without my link to the Earth providing more of a nuts-and-bolts perspective.

"Coming from the ancient world as I do, this is still hard to believe," said White Buffalo. "I used to think teepees and campfires were a wonder, the best that mankind could achieve. This puts that to shame."

With that, she wandered off to take in the view from other parts of the circular viewing deck, leaving me alone with Ebon.

"So." I tapped my fingers on the rail that followed the curve of the window. "It's about time we talked, don't you think?"

Ebon smiled at me. "About us, you mean? And what happened at the Berkeley Pit?"

I shook my head. "About the war-self. About why the Earth had to make a new one to replace me."

Ebon took a deep breath and let it out slowly. "It's complicated, Gaia. And, honestly, it isn't that relevant. All that really matters is that you're going to regain your mantle and save humanity."

"Oh, okay." I rolled my eyes. "So I should just shut up and do as I'm told, in other words?"

"That's not what I said."

"It's *exactly* what you said," I told him. "And it brings up another great question, now that you mention it. Let's say I somehow take back my powers and get the new war-self out of the picture. Even then, how the hell am I going to stop the entire *planet* from wiping out the human race? Does that sound even the *slightest* bit realistic?"

"There's more to it," said Ebon. "You're not alone in this. You need to have faith in the plan."

"Maybe if I knew what the plan *was...*"

Ebon turned and took my hand. "Please trust me, Gaia. There are reasons for everything we've set in motion."

I caught his gaze then and held it with my own. "You're not

using your special *trick*, are you? Your mind control technique that got us over the border? Because if you are, I *swear...*"

"No tricks, Gaia," said Ebon. "I wouldn't use them on you, even if I *could.*"

I listened, glad to hear him admit what I already suspected.

"They won't work on avatars...current or past," he said. "I don't know why. It's just the way it is."

I stared deep into his eyes but couldn't tell if he was lying. Maybe, in the end, it didn't matter. Either I bought into this, or I didn't.

That didn't mean I had to enjoy the constant evasions. "You said you were going to give me some answers, but you still haven't told me a damn thing."

"You're right." He squeezed my hand. "Okay, listen. I'll tell you what I know, and we'll just have to hope for the best, that it won't hurt the plan."

Just as he said those words, one of the big windows suddenly exploded inward, showering the viewing deck with shattered glass. A figure burst in through the opening, riding a chunk of stone that landed hard on the walkway.

Aside from the full-body black-leather jumpsuit, the figure looked just like me.

Breathing hard, she cast a fierce grin in my direction. She looked at me for all of a second, radiating hatred and scorn.

Then, she charged full-tilt right at me, hunks of the rock she'd ridden leaping up and whizzing along in her wake.

Spewing a howl of pure, primal fury, Gaia 2 raced toward me like Hell on two legs. Ebon didn't hesitate to intercept her, fists raised in readiness, but one of the rock shards flipped around from her wake and clocked him in the temple, sending him reeling.

With the seconds he'd bought, I ran—randomly, without any plan or options. It did no good, as more chunks of rock peppered my legs, taking me down. Just like that, she was towering over me with teeth clenched in a vicious grin.

"Hello, *bitch*." She kicked me hard in the side and laughed wickedly. "I guess you *blew* it, bitch."

Again, she pumped a hard-toed black leather boot into my side, making me cry out in pain.

"Please, stop!" I rolled away from the next kick and scrambled to my knees.

"Some replacement *you* are!" Gaia 2 snapped her fingers, and nearby hunks of rock popped up from the floor. They pulled together into a slab the size of my head, then zoomed over and crashed into my hip, slamming me back to the floor. "You aren't *fit* to live on the same *planet* as me!"

My deepening frown had nothing to do with the pain from her attack. "Replacement? What are you *talking* about?"

"Playing dumb again?" Gaia 2 fluttered her fingers, and the rock hunks popped up and spun around me—then shot inward all at once. "Or maybe you *are* just a moron. Either way, you need to be *put down.*"

She raised her arms, and the rock hunks levitated high above me, ready for a final assault. Before she could send them plunging down at me, though, they started shivering in midair, resisting her control.

Then, instead of bombarding me, they went after her. They pummeled her hard and repeatedly, sending her stumbling into the wall of the inner hub of the observation deck. It was then that I saw who'd been powerful enough to seize control of the pieces of rock from Gaia 2.

White Buffalo Calf Woman.

"Come with me, Gaia!" she shouted over Gaia 2's howls of pain.

Instead, I leaped up and tackled Gaia 2 against the wall, pinning her there with the force of my rage.

"Why did you *do* it? Why did you *kill* those women and *frame* me for the murders?"

"I know!" Gaia 2 laughed. "*Hilarious*, right?"

Up close, it was like looking in a mirror. She could not have *been* a more perfect twin. "How did you *find* me here?" I snapped.

"Like calls to like, bitch." She sneered and spat in my face. "You might drop off my radar now and then, but I *always* pick up your signal soon enough!"

"Who's the *stupid* one?" I pushed her harder against the wall. "You're *done* now. You're going *down.* You shouldn't have *come* here."

"Is that what you think?" She laughed louder than ever. "You think you've *beaten* me?"

Just then, I heard a loud rumbling, and the observation deck trembled under my feet. As Gaia 2 kept laughing, the whole tower swayed from side to side.

"You're an even *bigger* moron that I thought!" said Gaia 2. "I can't believe she *based* you on me!"

The ground continued to rumble, and the tower continued to sway. I had to shift my weight to stay on my feet as the whole thing teetered.

Suddenly, White Buffalo was by my side, gripping my arm. "Gaia, we have to leave. Let her go and come with me."

The tower's shaking intensified. So did Gaia 2's laughter.

"We must live to fight another day." White Buffalo's voice was insistent, as was her tight grip on my arm. "Come *now*."

"Use your power!" I told her. "Whatever she's doing, counteract it!"

"I already am." Her eyes flared, and I could suddenly see the strain in them. "*She* isn't the only one applying *pressure*." Her face twitched, and she grunted. "A much more *powerful* entity is doing most of the damage…one I cannot resist *alone*."

"Who?"

"*Mother Earth*, you dumb bitch!" said Gaia 2. "God! Do you have to have *everything* spelled out for you?"

Again, the shaking got worse. The deck tipped back and forth, making it harder than ever for me to stay standing.

As much as I hated to admit it, we couldn't win this fight.

"All right, fine!" I hauled back a fist, aiming it at Gaia 2's head. "Just give me a second!"

Ebon, who'd finally come around, grabbed my arm. "Leave her! We need to go!"

"She'll be a lot easier to carry if she's unconscious!"

He and White Buffalo pulled me away as the tower tipped farther than ever. "We're not taking her with us!" he said. "She'll point Mother Earth right at us!"

"She'll do that anyway!" I shouted as they swung me toward the open window.

"Not where we're going," hissed White Buffalo, right before she and Ebon leaped out of the window with me between them.

18

I have always been somewhat earthbound, it's true. Something to do with being an avatar of the planet; also, I'll admit, due to the complications of not having identification that would stand up to airport security. It comes with the territory when you're created supernaturally instead of being born the usual human being way.

But I finally got a taste of flight that night, as White Buffalo and Ebon carried me out into the sky over Vancouver.

Cool night air took my breath away as we hurtled into the very view we'd admired from the observation deck of the Vancouver Lookout. The city's towers glowed around us, window after window lit from within. Boats and ships in the harbor cast their beams upon the still and darkling waters, flowing out like mirages beyond their original sources. Lights glittered on the hillsides like stars fallen to Earth, blinking out their cries for rescue from the twinkling firmament above.

Immersed in it now, as we were, that scenery seemed so much sharper and more vibrant. So much more imminent and shocking. The wonders around us were more encompassing, more all-consuming—also more threatening. The gulf between us and the ground was vast; if we dropped, the distance would kill us in a matter of seconds.

Fortunately, the woman beside me was keeping us aloft and guiding us forward. Glowing with a shimmering incandescence,

White Buffalo propelled us from the Lookout and between the nearest buildings like birds in flight.

In the top floor windows of one of those buildings, I saw a cleaning lady watching and waving, sweeper nozzle in hand. I wanted to wave back but knew that if I did, I'd have to let go of the hand of the woman who was keeping me airborne—that, or the hand of the man who was holding on to her through me.

Slowly, we descended, following a long arc down to street level. As soon as our feet touched the sidewalk, White Buffalo stopped glowing and let go of my hand.

Looking back up into the sky, I saw no pursuers coming after us. "Nobody followed us," I said. "Looks like we're safe for now."

"Not as long as *she* knows where we are." White Buffalo pointed at the street, at the planet underneath. "We need some cover, Ebon."

"Coming right up." Ebon stood in the middle of the sidewalk, spread his arms wide, and closed his eyes. He remained quiet and mostly still for a long moment, the slight quivering of his fingers the only sign of movement.

Then, when I heard the sound of something squeaking nearby, he opened his eyes and lowered his arms. "Done and done, milady. I just called up some reinforcements, and they're here."

The squeaking got closer and seemed to be coming from all directions. Soon, the source of it became known to me as well, as the first of a legion of small, furry creatures emerged into the bright beams of the next streetlight along our way.

Rats.

A horde of them scampered up and surrounded us on all sides, retaining an untouched pocket for us even as they matched our pace and direction of travel.

"We have a screen from below now." Ebon gestured overhead, and a flock of bats gathered above us, also squealing and matching our speed and direction. "And one from above."

"Still," said White Buffalo. "It's safe to say our time here has expired. Even screened, as we are now, it's won't be long until the world and her warrior run us to ground."

"I agree," said Ebon. "They're too close. Even with my screens, they'll take us down soon enough."

"We need to leave tonight instead of tomorrow," said White Buffalo. "As soon as possible, we need to reach our destination, or all will be lost."

"It could be risky," said Ebon. "Remember, water plays havoc with my blocking techniques. We could end up *very* exposed."

"But we could also use the water in our defense," said White Buffalo. "Maybe we stand a chance as long as we're not on dry land."

"Maybe," said Ebon. "I can try screening us with fish and birds and see how that works out."

"What about the local Landkind?" asked White Buffalo. "Or are they all on Mother Earth's side?"

"That's a good question," said Ebon. "Maybe Mid can reach out to the Lady of the Strait of Georgia and find out."

"Our escape could be possible after all, in spite of the challenges."

Ebon blew out his breath as we rounded the corner, still surrounded by our shielding rats and bats. "I just hope we don't lead them right to where we're going."

"It doesn't matter if they follow us or not." White Buffalo patted his shoulder. "They can't reach us when we get inside."

"Where is this again?" I asked. "This place we're going?"

"You'll see, warrior." White Buffalo smiled. "I will tell you this, though—there is no other place like it in all the world."

We finally approached the familiar front door of our hotel. Dispersing his rats and bats with a flurry of flutters and squeaks, Ebon stormed up and grabbed the glass door's ornate brass handle.

"You two go up and get Mid," he said. "Make it snappy. I'll meet you all in the lobby after I take care of something."

"What's that?" I asked.

"Checking us out early," said Ebon, bowing slightly as he held the door open for White Buffalo and me. "Assuming Mid didn't empty the mini-bar, it should just take a minute," he said with a wink.

19

The four of us rushed along the marina pier, searching for the berth of the boat Ebon had rented. Thanks also to Ebon, someone was supposed to meet us there—though trusting her, trusting *anyone*, was taking a massive risk.

As we hurried over the wooden planks between rows of bobbing vessels, Mid suddenly stopped. "Did we lock the car? I was in so much of a rush, I don't remember."

Ebon laughed. He'd parked the Indiana State Police cruiser in a nearby lot, and he assured her no one would mess with it there. Even if they did, he doubted it would matter; it was possible none of us would come back from where we were going...and if we did, we'd have *much* bigger things to worry about.

As Ebon had been told when he'd made arrangements over the phone, our ride was at the very end of the pier—a small fishing boat with the name "Sea Lyin'" printed on the tail. Someone was already on board, waiting for us, and she leaned out and waved when she saw us coming.

Ebon waved back exuberantly. "Georgia, I presume?"

"None other." The woman aboard the boat was tall and slim with red hair cut in a bouncy bob. She wore a loose green blouse with the sleeves rolled up and high-waisted white slacks cinched with a gold chain belt. "You shouldn't have any trouble keeping *my* name 'strait.'" She giggled.

"Because you *are* a strait," said Ebon. "As in a body of water. Nice play on words!"

"Thank you!" Georgia fluttered her hands overhead as if to quiet a round of applause. "I'll be here all week! Please, try the veal!"

"You're too much, Georgia!" Laughing, Ebon gestured at the three of us. "I *know* you're going to hit it off with *this* bunch." He reached for Mid's hand and helped her step up on the gangplank. "This is Mid Silvergone, a classic Earth avatar and jailbreak expert. Mid, this is Georgia."

"Very nice to meet you," said Mid as Georgia helped her across the plank and into the boat.

"And this…" Ebon reached for White Buffalo's hand next. "…is White Buffalo Calf Woman, a powerful Native American goddess of the Midwest. She possesses astounding abilities…"

"But water isn't really her thing, right?" Smiling, Georgia led her onto the boat. "No sweat. I've got it covered. I'm not just here for my pretty face and awesome figure, you know."

Finally, Ebon reached for me. "And this is Gaia Charmer."

"Of course I know Gaia. The rightful current avatar of Mother Earth, recently deposed." Georgia curtsied. "It's my honor to work with you, ma'am."

"Thank you," I said as I crossed the gangplank. "It's good to meet you, too."

"Looking forward to doing some brainstorming about the future." Georgia helped me down into the boat and smiled excitedly. "Going from being a simple strait to embodying the entire *Pacific Ocean* will be a hell of a challenge! I'm going to need all the guidance I can get!"

I looked back at Ebon when I heard that one, and he just shrugged. He hadn't mentioned the full details of the deal it had taken to get Georgia to help us, but now I knew. Since we'd heard that most Landkind (and Waterkind) had sided with Gaia 2 and Mother Earth, it had taken the promise of a huge promotion—from being the avatar of a single strait to becoming the Pacific Ocean in human form—to get Georgia to throw in with our beleaguered little band.

Ebon took a last look around, scanning the sky as well as the shore, and then he joined us aboard the *Sea Lyin'.* "Let's get going." He untied the rope from the cleat on the pier and headed for the driver's seat up front. "The longer we sit around out here, the greater our chances of getting squashed like a bug by you-know-who."

He started the motor, pulled out of the slip, and headed out into the heart of the harbor. It was a warm summer night, and other boats were out there, too, but traffic wasn't bad.

Looking back, I saw there was more activity focused on the Vancouver Lookout. Helicopters circled the structure, whisking searchlights over its damaged and tipped observation deck. Fire ladders stretched up from below, reaching partway up the tower's height in the red and blue strobes of emergency responder lights. I could hear voices calling out from that direction over loudspeakers, muffled by distance.

It was just another mess left in the wake of my wicked twin.

"Are the screens up?" I asked over the thrum of the boat's motor. "Are we blocking her?"

"I'm doing the best I can," Ebon said over his shoulder. "I've got a huge school of fish running under us, and a swarm of gnats over-head—but like I told you, the water interferes with my blocking. We all need to be ready for anything."

Mid closed her eyes, tipped her head back, and spread her arms. "I'll let you know if I detect anyone closing in."

"Dry land is my usual battlefield," said White Buffalo, "but I'll do what I can to repel any attackers."

"Don't worry so much, people." As Georgia spoke, streams of water rose from the strait around us, meeting above her head to form the twin-lobed outline of a heart. "I've got this. The entire Strait of Georgia and all its associated waters and contents stand ready to defend you with unparalleled power and ferocity."

Her confidence was reassuring, to a point—though I doubted a single body of water could stand for long against the combined strength of Mother Earth and Gaia 2.

"White Buffalo." Ebon turned from the controls and tapped her shoulder. "I need you to make sure we stay on course. You're the only one who knows exactly how to get where we're going."

White Buffalo approached him. "I will gladly steer us there."

"Be my guest." Ebon moved out of the way, relinquishing the wheel to her steady hands. "If anything seems off, let me know immediately."

"I wouldn't dream of doing otherwise." As soon as she took the wheel, White Buffalo eased the boat to starboard, adjusting its heading.

"So, where exactly are we going, anyway?" asked Georgia. "You haven't been very specific about that."

"Someplace amazing," said Ebon. "One of the few places in the world that even the world itself doesn't know is there."

Georgia frowned. "Which is…?"

"You'll see soon enough." Ebon turned to White Buffalo. "How long will it take to get there, do you think?"

She thought for a moment. "Three hours, perhaps more. It's hard to say, especially with the time differential when we cross the border."

"The border of what?" said Georgia. "There's nothing three hours out except open ocean."

"Nothing you know of," said White Buffalo.

"Wow," said Georgia. "Nothing like heading out to sea and not getting a straight answer about what we're *looking* for."

"Welcome to *my* world," I told her.

Shaking her head, she came over to stand beside me, watching the lights of the city recede behind us. "They aren't telling you anything either, huh? Aren't you the one who's supposed to save the human race from extinction?"

"Apparently." I shrugged. "Though that's pretty much all I know at this point."

"Does that sound like a recipe for success to you?" Smirking, she pulled out a vaping pen and switched it on. "Keeping your key people in the dark?"

"Sure, but what do I know?" I smirked, too, and tugged on my braid. "I'm just a former human avatar of Mother Earth, that's all."

Georgia laughed. "Seriously? Because I *thought* you looked familiar."

"Yep." I nodded. "But now I'm just the least powerful person in the boat, wondering what the hell I've gotten myself into."

"Let me tell you something." She moved closer and lowered her voice. "Something I've learned after all my years as a body of water between Vancouver Island and the mainland of British Columbia."

"What's that?"

"The people who think they've got it all under control? They end up the same way as everyone else when they fall in the deep end."

"How is that?" I asked.

Georgia grinned slyly. "All wet."

For the next few hours, the five of us were mostly quiet as we rode onward, the sound of the boat's motor and the lapping of waves against the hull the only things audible. Those sounds and the rocking motion of the boat were almost hypnotic out there in the darkness, putting me in a frame of mind that was strangely calm and contemplative considering the level of danger we faced.

I found myself thinking not of what lay ahead, but what I'd left behind. I wondered if my friends back in Confluence were okay, and if they'd all recovered from Gaia 2's attack. Were Duke, Luna, Nephelae, Ashanti, and the others safe and sound? Were they thinking of me?

I especially wondered about Briar. Was he working the case, reaching out to law enforcement across the country to try to bring me in to stand trial? Was he slow-walking the investigation to give me time to resolve it myself?

Did he miss me?

Looking across the boat, I watched the breeze ruffle Ebon's hair, and I remembered his kiss. It shouldn't have meant a thing to me; he was practically a stranger, and I didn't appreciate the way he kept me in the dark about the "secret plan" and our mysterious destination. So why did I still wonder about him? Why did I care even the slightest bit about how he felt about me?

And why would I give him even a second thought if there was a chance he might be influencing my mind with his powers?

The hell if I knew.

"Something's coming!"

At the sound of Mid's cry, I snapped out of my reverie and shot to full attention. My romantic concerns—or lack thereof—would have to wait.

"Damnit." Ebon leaped to the back of the boat and stared into the inky blackness behind us. "I thought we were in the clear."

"You thought wrong, hon!" Mid's voice was thick with tension. "The war-self is out there, coming in fast."

"Skimming the surface on a big pebble, no doubt," said Ebon. "Or a slate surfboard."

Just as the words left his mouth, the hum of a high-performance engine rose in the distance. Even from so far away, I could tell it put our measly motor to shame.

"Try a speedboat, heading right for us." Though we were long out of her strait, Georgia still communed with and controlled the waters to some extent. Her sensitivity weakened the further we went from the strait, but she still had a handle on local phenomena.

"Shit." Ebon played with the controls, but we knew we were already going as fast as we could. "How much farther until we reach the Niche?"

My ears perked up. It was the first I'd heard anyone mention that word.

"We are close," said White Buffalo. "It could be a few minutes from now...or many."

"But you can *feel* it nearby?" asked Ebon.

"I feel it...somewhere up ahead." White Buffalo took a deep breath, let it out slowly. Her hands tightened on the wheel. "The Niche is always in flux. That is how it escapes detection." She sounded strained. "But it also makes it difficult for me to locate with precision."

Ebon fell silent, gazing into the darkness. Georgia and I stood beside him and followed his gaze. There was no visible sign of the speedboat, but the sound of it continued to grow closer.

"How long until the boat reaches us, Mid?" he asked over his shoulder.

"Not long," she told him. "Minutes. Maybe ten, maybe five."

"All right then." He turned to Georgia. "This is why we brought you along."

"Well, I'm up for anything," she said, "but you should know, I don't pack the same punch I did back in the actual strait. The waters out here seem to be compliant, but keep in mind, they're primarily controlled by other entities."

"You can negotiate with them, though," said Ebon.

"What do you think I've been doing on the ride out?" Georgia tapped the side of her head with a fingertip. "Sweet-talking all the way, baby—but Waterkind can be pretty unpredictable. We flow where we wanna flow, know what I mean?" She rolled her hands through the air like rippling water.

"Just do your best. That's all we can ask." Ebon nodded. "Hopefully, if that's the war-self, she'll be limited, too. We're in deep waters out here. The nearest dirt and rock are a long way down."

"Dredging anything up will take a lot of effort." I spoke from experience, with authority. Nobody knew her powers and limitations better. "Then she has to propel it in our direction. She'll be struggling."

"You should worry more about Mother Earth herself," said White Buffalo. "She could open a maw in the sea floor with a thought and swallow us up like *that*." She snapped her fingers.

"Let's hope it doesn't come to that." Ebon rushed over to her side at the wheel. "Steady as she goes."

The sound of the speedboat was swiftly becoming a roar. The *Sea Lyin'* kept plowing ahead, but it was obvious our pursuer was closing the gap.

No one asked White Buffalo how far we were from the Niche. We'd know when we got there, *if* we got there.

"I see it." Georgia pointed into the distance astern, which still looked pitch black to me. "It's right—"

Suddenly, something flew past my head at a high rate of speed, and Ebon cried out behind me. I turned to see him double over with a grimace, clutching his gut.

Blood seeped out between his fingers as he sucked in air between clenched teeth.

"What the hell?" I ran over and caught him as he slumped to the deck. "What was *that?*"

"Maybe our girl decided to try some good, old-fashioned *firearms* instead of struggling to dredge up the ocean bottom," said Georgia.

Just then, another projectile whizzed past and punched a hole in the cowling around the steering column. White Buffalo whipped around, hands glowing, and caught the next one in midair before it could puncture anyone or anything else.

"Not a gun." I looked up at the polished little object as it bobbed between her hands, afloat in a field of golden energy. "A *stone*. She doesn't *need* to dredge up ammo…she brought *her own*."

Another pebble shot into the boat and through the floor, followed by a glancing shot off the port metal railing. Even as the fusillade continued, Georgia stood fearlessly in the rear of the boat, head down and arms outstretched with palms facing the enemy. Glittering swirls of energy danced around her hands, threading back and forth in a kind of glowing cat's cradle. The number of threads built and the light they shed increased, giving off a throbbing hum…

Then, Georgia flung the gathered cradle into the water and tossed her head back with a loud howl. The water where she'd thrown the cradle sparked and bubbled—and then a wave surged up, higher than her head, racing away from the *Sea Lyin'*.

"Take that!" she shouted. "Good luck not getting swamped when *that* hits ya'!"

But Georgia's wave didn't deter our pursuer. The roar of the engine continued to climb as the speedboat raced nearer.

Then, Mid cried out with sudden alarm. "The boat is a decoy! She's *on top of us!*"

I looked up in time to see a cloud of dark soot part overhead, revealing my twin gliding above the boat. As the soot parted, she dropped down at us, grinning wickedly.

Georgia gave up on her wave, letting it slump back into the sea, and swung around to lash out with a jet of seawater that slammed into Gaia 2's chest. The impact threw my twin into the ocean with a splash, some distance from the boat.

"White…Buffalo!" Ebon gasped out the words. "Did we…*miss* it…somehow?"

"No!" she shouted. "We're *close*. I can *feel* it!"

Something collided with the underside of our boat, then, and it rocked violently to port. There was another strike from below within seconds, and the *Sea Lyin'* bounced heavily to starboard.

As this was happening, I finally glimpsed the speedboat approaching through the darkness. The craft rocketed toward us, its pilot visible in the glow of the controls in the cockpit.

It only took a moment for me to recognize Beatrice Brown, the old woman I'd rescued from the cinder block pile in the basement of murder victim Imogene Parker. She was easily in her 80s and not in any better shape than Mid, but she was driving that speedboat like a maniac with mad skills.

As I tried to adjust to the thought of her presence so far from Confluence, the *Sea Lyin'* rocked again from another underwater strike. The jarring movement made Ebon shout in agony, unable to stop himself from reacting.

Arms swung out, Georgia made the water leap away on either side of our boat, opening up deep trenches that flanked the single narrow path we skimmed down the middle. But it took only a moment for the impacts to continue as strong as ever.

Then, a single hand sprang up from the water and latched onto the side of the boat like a grappling hook. Gaia 2 was coming aboard.

No one else saw Gaia 2's hand on the edge of the boat. Powerless as I was, dealing with her was up to me.

Leaving Ebon on the deck, I jumped up and darted over to the starboard side of the boat. As I did, a second hand joined the first.

By the time I got there, the top of her head was rising between those hands. Her eyes met mine, brimming with evil intent.

At which point, I hauled up a foot to kick her loose and brought it down hard on the fingers of her right hand. She yowled in pain, and I prepared to kick the left hand, too.

That was when the *Sea Lyin'* started spinning, inexplicably.

The air filled with whirling, flashing streamers, and the water around us fell skyward as upside-down rain showers. A continuous roar of thunder blasted from all directions, nearly deafening.

Then, even as the rain fell up from the ocean's surface, thousands of stars fell down from the sky, which was blazing with fire.

Distracted by the show, I missed my twin as she swung herself, using the boat's spin for momentum, and flung a leg up high enough to hook over the railing. I looked back just as she was hauling herself the rest of the way over and into the boat.

Heart pounding, I grabbed hold of her arm and prepared to toss her back overboard. She fought me, oblivious to the insanity that was going on around us.

Multicolored fireworks exploded in the sky, showering the

seascape with sparks that didn't go dark when they hit the water. Weird creatures with spiny black wings and mangled, glistening faces flapped around us, shrieking over the thunder.

Gathering my strength for one last effort, I let up just enough that my surge, when it came, would surprise her. The two of us grappled in the flashing, seething light, fighting the spin of the boat as well as each other.

Just as I was ready to make my big push, everything came to a crashing halt. The *Sea Lyin'* stopped spinning and dropped down hard, sending everyone tumbling out of the boat.

The fireworks, thunder, upside-down rain, and spiny black creatures disappeared all at once. For that matter, so did the ocean depths.

Shaking off the shock and sitting up, I saw that we were somewhere unknown—a black sand beach rimmed with huts built of clay, with ragged-looking thatched roofs. The clay was as gray as the mid-day sky overhead, which was blanketed with low, dark clouds.

Somehow, we had gone instantly from pitch darkness in the middle of the night to a cloudy afternoon with ample daylight.

Gaia 2 and I took in the scene with everyone else, but her reaction was much different from mine. Even as I puzzled over the nature of our whereabouts, she flung her arms wide, trying to put the local materials to use—no doubt to kill the rest of us.

But nothing happened. The black sand didn't stir. No chunks of clay burst free of the huts and shot over to pound us. The ground didn't rumble or split open to swallow us up.

Her face flushed with rage, she continued to pose and reach, refusing to give up. Unlike the middle of the ocean, this new place had plenty of the materials she needed to make the most of her powers.

Still, the ground resisted her. Not so much as a grain of black sand danced at her command.

"Give it up!" I told her. "Obviously, you have as much power as *I* do around here."

Hateful eyes locked on me, she continued to strain, to no avail.

I, on the other hand, had other fish to fry. Turning, I headed back to Ebon's side, flipping her the bird along the way.

All our crew were injured or in shock, but Ebon was in the worst shape by far. Sprawled in the wreckage of the *Sea Lyin'*, he sweated and shivered and groaned. His hands and torso were soaked with red, and his skin was ashen pale from blood loss.

I dropped to my knees beside him and tore open his shirt, exposing the wound. Otherwise, I was completely at a loss as to what to do. My expertise had always tended toward geology; performing first aid on someone was not remotely in my wheelhouse.

As a supernatural being, he should have been able to heal himself, I thought—but that wasn't happening. Maybe the same effect that robbed Gaia 2 of her powers in this place was tamping down his own extraordinary abilities.

Whatever the reason, it looked to me like the extinctionist was about to become extinct.

Looking around, I saw Georgia stirring on the black sand near the boat, looking reasonably undamaged.

"Georgia!" I gestured hurriedly. "Ebon's in bad shape!"

She sat up, rubbing her head, and looked my way—then out to sea. I guessed she was testing her powers, the same as Gaia 2…and as the moment ticked away, she looked deeply annoyed.

"I'm no good to him, Gaia," she said. "I've got no control over the waters here."

"Come here, anyway!" I told her. "He needs first aid!"

Georgia scrambled over to join me. "He needs more than that," she said darkly. "A *lot* more."

"Damnit." I knew she was right. "Shit!"

There was one more hope, I thought, one among us who might not have lost her powers. "White Buffalo?" I looked around and spotted her leaning against the splintered hull of the boat. She had cuts and bruises on her face and arms but luckily was in one piece and alert. "Ebon's hurt! Can you do anything?"

Just as she shook her head, I heard Mid cry out nearby…then Gaia 2 shouting for attention.

"Imposter! Surrender now!"

Turning, I saw that Gaia 2 had her arm wrapped tightly around Mid's throat—and a rock in her free hand, clutched above Mid's forehead. Even without her powers, the first thing the war witch had grabbed as a weapon was a piece of the Earth's substance she was so used to manipulating.

"Surrender or I'll kill the old woman!" Gaia 2 shook the rock for emphasis. Mid's terrified eyes were fixed on it as it came closer to her head. "Don't make *her* pay the price that *you* owe, traitor!"

"Let her go." I got to my feet and started toward them. "Don't hurt her."

"She deserves it, actually," snapped Gaia 2. "You'd be rotting in prison right now if not for her! And this little band of yours wouldn't be opposing Mother Earth's survival protocol!"

"None of us opposes her survival," I said. "We love this world with all our hearts. But we also believe there's a better way for her to survive than exterminating billions of human beings."

"I don't *care* what you believe! Neither does *she!* If she did, *I* wouldn't be standing here. I wouldn't be needed to *replace* my *replacement.*"

"Wow." I stopped halfway toward them. "That's the second time you've called me your *replacement.*"

Gaia 2 laughed. "You mean nobody *told* you?"

I spread my arms. "Told me what?"

"That I was the *original* war-self," said Gaia 2. "Mother Earth brought me to life all the way back in *1947.*"

My arms fell to my sides. I remembered seeing a photo that

looked just like me in one of Ellie Grenoble's scrapbooks. *Gaia Charmer Grenoble, 23, of Confluence,* the caption had read…and something else besides, which I recited aloud. "'Reported missing on Friday, June 6, 1947.'"

"Give the girl a kewpie doll!" Again, she laughed. "That's when I went missing, all right. I was carrying out my mission just fine, working to wipe out humanity and save the planet from their precious atom bombs—but certain *bitches* didn't appreciate my work! They got the jump on me and put me away where even Big Mama Earth couldn't find me!"

I frowned, trying to wrap my head around what she'd said. "And you're saying I *replaced* you? But I wasn't created for *decades.*"

"Exactly!" said Gaia 2. "Nuclear weapons didn't lead to planetary destruction after all. Then *climate change* became enough of a threat to convince Big Mama she needed a new *war bitch* for a new *age.*" She sneered, baring her teeth over Mid's shoulder. "Too bad you came out *watered down* this time."

Just then, Georgia spoke up. "Ebon is dying! The bleeding won't stop!"

I'd been fixated on the answers Gaia 2 was doling out, but I shot my focus back to Ebon. "White Buffalo!" I shouted. "What can we do to save his life?"

I looked back and saw her standing over him, jaws clenched as she gazed down at his wound. Of all of us, she seemed to know this place best, whatever it was; I thought she stood the best chance of coming up with a solution.

She said nothing for a moment…then gathered herself up and marched away from us. I called her name, but she ignored me, just kept heading for the thatched huts along the treeline.

"Hey!" hollered Gaia 2. "Doesn't anyone care that I'm about to kill your *friend* here?"

I watched as White Buffalo stooped to enter one of the huts, disappearing inside. Then, I turned back to Ebon and Georgia, then finally back to my twin.

"Can't this whole hostage situation wait till things settle down some?" I asked. "Can we just…pick it up later? I've got a dying man over here, and I can't deal with two life-or-death scenarios at the same time."

Gaia 2 unleashed a howl of unfettered rage that made Mid wince. "*No*, this hostage situation *can't* wait! In fact, I'm going to snap this bitch's neck right *now.*"

Before she could carry out her threat, though, another voice called out from the water. "Help me! Somebody help me!"

Looking toward the voice, I saw Beatrice Brown trapped under the upended speedboat she'd been driving during the battle. The waterlogged old woman clawed at the black sand as the surf continued to rise around her.

Without a word, Gaia 2 released Mid and ran to help her partner. Grunting, she lifted the boat off Beatrice, then scooped her up and marched out of the surf with her in her arms.

It was then that I saw White Buffalo emerge from the hut. "Everyone!" she shouted through cupped hands. "The Ancestrum has awakened!"

As she said it, a tall, slender woman with long chestnut hair stepped out of the hut behind her. She wore an ankle-length white shift, and her feet were bare.

White Buffalo pointed, and the woman hurried over to Ebon's side. Pushing her hair behind her ears, she crouched and held her flattened hand over his wound. Ebon groaned and writhed but didn't open his eyes.

When the woman spoke, her voice was raspy, as if she hadn't used it in a long time. "He will fail soon," she said.

"Please help him!" My concern for him welled up within me, more compelling than I'd expected. "Please save him if you can!"

The woman looked up at me. "Use of the powers of the Mother is forbidden in this place. It is the only way to keep it secret as we do." She sighed. "Each time we open the channel and reach outside the Niche to tap those powers, we risk discovery."

"This man is worth it." Mid looked haggard as she approached, rubbing her throat. "You do realize he's the Extinctionist, don't you, Drusilla?"

Drusilla looked surprised. "The ender of species?" Her expression turned to one of worry. "Has he come for *us?*"

Mid shook her head. "He's a good man, Drusilla…an ally in our struggle. We need him to see this thing through."

Again, Drusilla raised her hands over Ebon's wound, and her face darkened. "Not much time left until *his own* extinction now."

"Then do it," said Mid. "In the name of our order, please save him."

Drusilla got to her feet. "But our order is not pledged to support your struggle, whatever it is. Why should we take this terrible chance if we might yet declare our opposition to your efforts?"

"Enough." Mid turned away, facing the line of huts atop the beach. "Sisters of the Ancestrum! Come save this man's life, I beseech you! Come in all your numbers and work miracles as you did in days of old!"

2 3

Nothing moved among those huts but the stirring of the wind. Though I didn't know who occupied them, what the Ancestrum was or why they were there, I silently prayed that they would soon emerge and do something to rescue Ebon.

Silent moments passed. Finally, the huts gave up their inhabitants. Women stepped out of them, yawning and stretching and rubbing their eyes. They all wore the same white shifts, but they looked quite different from each other—some tall, some short, some black, some white, some blonde, some brunette, some thin, some fat, some young, some old. Their hair, when long, was mussed and tangled, their shifts wrinkled from too long in repose.

There must have been huts in the forest, too, for more women strolled out of the treeline, also sleepy and clad in white. They milled around with the others, dozens gathered at the fringe of the beach, looking in our direction…and then they started toward us.

"See?" Mid smiled gravely. "I knew they were listening."

The women encircled us, staring at Ebon, their expressions unreadable.

"Thank you all for coming." Mid gestured at Ebon. "Please save him."

A slender woman with long black hair stepped forward, hands folded over her belly. "We don't object to the saving of lives, but Drusilla is right about the danger of channeling power from the

109

world beyond. Our Niche is only safe as long as it remains hidden from Mother."

"Tess is right," said a short redhead with eyes like shining emeralds. "*But*...what if he's meant to play a vital role in something that's of great interest to us?"

"He is!" said Mid. "We've come because Mother is about to *massacre* all humanity, and this man, Ebon, can help us stop her!"

The women of the Ancestrum murmured among themselves at that, looking concerned.

"That's right," said Mid. "Mother Earth is determined to finish them off this time! And she brought back her nastiest *war bitch* to do it!" She pointed down the beach at the surf, where Gaia 2 was in the process of working on the speedboat while Beatrice sat on the black sand away from the water and watched. "Remember *her?*"

Again, there was murmuring among the women.

When it stopped, Tess nodded at Drusilla. "We should do it. If the stakes are that high, we should take the chance."

Drusilla still didn't look happy. "And if Mother finds us? What hope will we have then? What hope will there be for *humanity?*"

"The same as there is now!" I said, sick of listening to their debate while Ebon died. "*Zero hope!* So what do you have to lose?"

Tess looked at me as if seeing me for the first time. "A *second* war-self? What's going on here?"

"I'll explain later!" snapped Mid.

"It's about time," I said.

Mid scowled at Tess, then Drusilla. "Just save him, *please.*"

There was a quiet, tense moment. Drusilla looked around at the crowd—and every woman thrust her right fist up in the air. The vote was unanimous.

"All right." Drusilla crouched beside Ebon, placing her hands on his blood-soaked wound. "Let's get this done."

The women all held hands. Tess, at the front of the group, reached down and placed her free hand on Drusilla's head.

"Make it as quick as we can," said Tess. "Reach out, get what we need, and slam the door shut behind us. Don't give Mother enough time to find her way into the Niche."

The women of the Ancestrum all closed their eyes, bowed their heads, and fell silent. None of the rest of us interrupted them, either…though Gaia 2 kept banging away at the speedboat. From a distance, I couldn't tell if she was trying to fix something or tear something out of the damaged craft.

The Ancestrum swayed rhythmically, synchronized perfectly. As I watched, they started to glow with a soft, golden light.

As the tempo of their swaying increased, the glow built also, rising in brightness. Faster and faster they swayed…brighter and brighter they glowed…

Until all of them suddenly flung up their hands, still joined, and froze.

It was then that the gray clouds opened directly overhead, revealing a starry night sky. A blazing shower of white light slashed down from the opening, engulfing the women of the Ancestrum.

They all quivered at once in that pulsating wave, galvanized. Then they swung their hands down, and the light poured out of them, rushing through Tess's hand into Drusilla's head…and on into Ebon.

Surging with golden fire, he twisted on the black sand, making a choking sound. Suddenly, he lunged up, his bloody midsection off the ground while his shoulders and feet stayed down. Golden tendrils swirled around his wound, weaving in and out of the punctured gut with incredible speed.

The light flared then, obscuring his physical form in a burst of radiance. For a moment, I couldn't see him at all…just Drusilla's arms reaching into the flare, her hands as lost in the brilliance as he was.

And then I heard it. From within the flare, I heard a sound that made my heart beat faster.

He took a breath.

The second that gasp happened, Tess broke contact with Drusilla, Drusilla let go of Ebon, and all the women of the Ancestrum followed suit. The light drained from everyone, and the hole in the sky sealed instantly.

As Ebon's body slumped to the sand, I could see his clothes were still bloody, but his gut was sealed. The wound was gone as if it has never been there.

They had *saved* him.

"What the *hell?*" Ebon sat up, then grimaced and clutched his belly. Though his wound was repaired, the pain was apparently still abundant.

I knelt beside him. "You were shot just before we entered the Niche. The Ancestrum healed you."

"At great personal risk," Drusilla said emphatically. "And the possible ruination of everything you see before you."

"I feel like I should apologize." Ebon chuckled, then gasped in pain. "Sorry for…surviving…"

"Save it for when Mother Earth obliterates us all in a fit of rage," said Drusilla.

"But if I wait till then…we'll all be dead…right?" He smirked through the pain. "So I'll just say it now…so we're all covered." He cleared his throat. "Sorry for getting us…obliterated by Mother Earth…whoever you are."

"Okay," said Drusilla. "And *you're welcome* for all of us saving your life."

She started to get up, and he caught her wrist. "Thank you," he said sincerely, gazing into her eyes…and then he looked around at the Ancestrum encircling us. "And thank all of you, too…from the bottom of my almost-dead heart."

24

It didn't feel like the middle of July in the Niche. There was a bite in the air, and the lack of direct sunlight kept things from warming up. Walking through the shade of the forest, I couldn't help shivering, especially when we were near streams or under the thickest cover.

Maeve, the emerald-eyed redhead who served as my guide, didn't seem the slightest bit bothered by it, though. She wore the light white shift that passed for a uniform in that place, but the thin garment might as well have been a snowsuit for all that the cold affected her.

"Is it always like this here?" I zipped up my leather jacket to ward off the chill as we walked between walls of dripping wet rock. "Doesn't it ever heat up?"

Maeve smiled and shook her head. She seemed like a sweet girl, and I was glad she'd volunteered to give me the nickel tour of the Niche. "It's always the same."

"No seasons?"

Again, she shook her head. "It's the best we could do when we made it." She had a lilt in her voice when she spoke, an accent that sounded Irish to me. "I mean, *I* didn't make it, I didn't exist yet— but those earliest forebears among us, it was the best they could manage." She stopped to smell a gray-petaled flower on a vine. "And we are *lucky* to have it."

I just nodded and followed her along the path. I intended to learn everything I could from her…and I was sure she planned to do the same with me.

She'd been assigned by the Ancestrum to show me around in the wake of the chaos on the beach, leading me off while Mid, White Buffalo, and Georgia stayed behind to oversee Ebon's recuperation. Maybe Maeve was also supposed to buy time before whatever was coming next. Maybe the Ancestrum needed time to think about how to approach the situation…though it didn't seem to me that it should take any time at all to decide whether or not to save humankind.

"So, who were they?" I asked as we stepped over a trickling stream. "Who were the earliest forebears who made this place?"

"The first of the avatars, brought to life in the very earliest days of humankind." Maeve grinned. "You can meet them later and ask about it yourself, if you like."

"Wait," I said. "Do you mean to tell me that the *first* Earth avatars in human form are *here?*"

"They *all* are," she told me. "When their time was up, and Mother had created new avatars to replace them, they came here to this hidden place to commune with each other. They came here to ensure their hard-won knowledge and wisdom would not be lost to the ages." She raised her eyebrows. "And they came here in case there was a crisis so extreme that their combined power might be needed to avert it."

"So you're saying *all* of you are here?" I asked. "Every single one of you since the dawn of humanity?"

She nodded. "Every avatar ever created—well, *almost* every avatar—is right here in the Niche. Together, they represent tens of thousands of years of Earth-human history."

I stopped on the path, stunned by what I was hearing. "They're all still *alive?*"

Maeve flattened her hand and tipped it from side to side. "*Not quite dead* might be more accurate."

We continued onward, winding between gray-trunked trees with odd-shaped pale green leaves I couldn't identify. I didn't see or hear any birds or animals at all, as if they, like the seasons, had been left out of the Niche's design.

"What do you mean by 'not quite dead?'" I asked.

"We're not truly immortal. We only have a *little* life left in us." She pinched a thumb and forefinger close to signify a tiny amount. "We use some of it when we're needed for something big. The rest of the time, we're fast asleep in dreamland, saving our energy."

"Until someone barges in and wakes you up," I said, "like us."

"Rude." She cast a disapproving glare my way that I could tell wasn't meant to be taken seriously. "And I was having such a sweet dream, too."

I laughed, enjoying her company in spite of the grave situation hanging over us.

"You weren't supposed to get here so soon yourself, you know," she told me. "That is to say, *all* avatars come here eventually, but you still have so much *life* ahead of you." She cleared her throat. "Hopefully, I mean."

"I didn't even know about this place until recently." I spread my arms to take in our surroundings.

"Well, as I understand it, you're sort of a special case," said Maeve. "I guess that's why you never got the full set of instructions like the rest of us."

"Full set?" I snorted. "I don't have *any* set, apparently." I let my arms fall hard against my sides. "I used to *think* I knew who I was, but I guess I knew *nothing* about myself this whole time."

"The whole war-self thing? Is that what you're talking about?" she asked.

"That's *part* of it," I said. "According to my genocidal *twin,* not only am I Mother Earth's war-self, but I'm a *replacement* for *her*... and now *she's* replaced *me*."

Maeve tipped her head to the side and scrunched up her eyes. "It does sound confusing when you put it like that."

"You *think* so?" I blew out my breath in frustration. "It's been making me *crazy*, finding out my whole life has been a lie."

"Well...not your *whole* life, right? I mean, you're still the same person inside, aren't you? No matter who they *say* you are."

I thought about it. "I guess so."

"Then what does it matter?" Maeve smiled as she answered her own question. "It doesn't. Not one damn bit."

I glared at her. "You're trying to get out of telling me, aren't you?"

She frowned. "Telling you what?"

"The truth. You're part of the Ancestrum, and you know the truth, but you don't want to tell me, do you? You're just like everyone else, aren't you?"

"The answer to your first question is no. I have no problem with telling you the truth. As for your second question—*hell, no!* Don't you *dare* compare me to everyone else!" She swatted me playfully on the arm.

"Then tell me," I said. "If you don't have a problem with telling me the truth, just do it."

Maeve led me through a low-hanging tangle of vines, then stopped at the edge of a sudden drop-off. Stepping up beside her, I found myself gazing down at a deep ravine full to bursting with greenery that swayed and fluttered in the afternoon breeze.

"Beautiful," I said softly. "Just beautiful."

"And yet," said Maeve, "one step in the wrong direction would be disastrous." She nodded knowingly. "Such is the life of the powerful. It's easy to go too far."

I thought for a moment. "You're talking about the first war-self?"

She shook her head. "I'm talking about Mother Earth."

We were both silent for a moment, the rattle of the leaves far below the only sound in our ears.

"It started after World War II," she said. "Humanity tore themselves to ribbons, and Mother turned a blind eye—until the atomic bomb. That weapon, she realized, could eventually ruin even her. The power at its core, fully evolved and misused by mankind, could kill not just them, but her."

I nodded grimly as she went on with the story.

"Mother decided the avatar at the time was not up to the task of stopping the humans from destroying her. *I* wasn't up to that task." She gave me a meaningful look, her emerald eyes forlorn, and shrugged. "I didn't have the heart to do what Mother demanded, which was to massacre every man, woman, and child on the planet. To clear the slate so she could be safe and start over.

"*That* is why she decided to bring the war-self to life," continued

Maeve. "Gaia Grenoble was her name. A more vicious, conscience-less bitch I could never imagine."

Again, I nodded. The date of the photo in Ellie's scrapbook agreed with the timeframe of Maeve's story.

"Gaia was the most powerful avatar ever created," said Maeve. "She was primed to wipe out humanity on Mother's order. Maybe she would've wiped *me* out, too, but I made it to the Niche before she could…and I told the Ancestrum what was happening.

"They were *unanimous* in their condemnation. Not *one* of them approved of Mother's mass-murder plan. Humanity had just fought the greatest war in history. We all agreed they deserved the chance to dig out of the rubble and start over…to *prove* themselves worthy of survival.

"For the first time in millennia, at the risk of discovery and attack by Mother Earth, the Ancestrum took action. They sent a team beyond the Niche—Tess, Drusilla, and I—imbued with communal power and loyal to the cause of saving humanity.

"Our team ambushed Gaia Grenoble and imprisoned her deep inside the Niche, in a cell that nullified her powers. We couldn't bring ourselves to execute a sister avatar, no matter what she'd done."

"And Mother didn't find out about this?" I asked.

"Oh, she was furious," said Maeve, "but she didn't know who'd done it, and she didn't know where to find Gaia Grenoble…so, eventually, she had to let it pass. She gave up the plan to wipe out humanity and moved on."

"But why didn't she just whip up a new war-self?"

"She waited because she still wasn't sure what had happened to the *last* one," explained Maeve. "The nuclear threat seemed to diminish, so she waited until the next sign of great crisis. That turned out to be *climate change*, another threat to the world as we know it.

"Just as before, Mother brought a war-self to life. The first one had been so *perfect*, she copied it exactly…but we were ready for her this time. We'd been watching from the Niche, waiting for this to happen, and we had a plan.

"Instead of abducting and locking away another war-self, possibly bringing ourselves to Mother's attention, we carefully reached out from the Niche and *changed* her. During her formative early days, we surrounded her with positive influences, including one in particular—a golem with a heart so bright and generous, it drove out much of the darkness in her soul. He became her moon."

"Duke," I said. "You're talking about Duke."

Maeve nodded. "It worked, too. She...*you*...became a being of compassion instead of hatred. You saw the good in humanity and would never obliterate them. Mother came to realize she had lost you.

"And *that* was when she found out *we* were to blame, and the first war-self was still buried deep inside the world, waiting to be set free."

"How was that possible?" I scowled. "As *careful* and *paranoid* as the Ancestrum is, how could Mother find out?"

Maeve sighed and shook her head. "Because we were betrayed from within. Some of us don't agree that humanity should be spared. They were informed by one of Gaia Grenoble's staunchest allies, the female golem who served as her original moon, much like your own Duke. Her name is Beatrice Brown."

So Beatrice was Gaia's moon, and a golem to boot. It explained her fierce dedication...and her survival under the pile of cinderblocks at Imogene's murder scene.

"Beatrice tipped off Gaia Grenoble's allies in the Ancestrum, and they took steps to advance their goals in support of humanity's extinction," said Maeve.

"What exactly did they do?" I asked.

"They freed Gaia Grenoble and returned her to Mother Earth," Maeve said darkly. "They turned her loose in the outside world."

"What then? Did they go with her?"

"No," said Maeve. "They're still here in the Niche. And they'll be among those who judge you at the trial."

"Wait, what?" I gaped at her, surprised. "I'm going to be *judged*? What the hell *for*?"

"Not just you. *Both* of you. Both Gaias. The Ancestrum will judge which of you is most worthy...which of your causes is most righteous. Your fates will rest on that decision, and so will the future of all humankind."

I returned my gaze to the ravine, feeling blindsided. Had Mid expected this when she'd brought me to the Niche? Was this why she hadn't told me more about our mission—because she'd always known I'd think it sounded like bullshit? The longshot of all longshots? Because maybe, if I'd known more of the truth, I wouldn't have agreed to come?

For that matter, what about all the other evasions in my life, all the outright lies? If what Maeve had told me was true, my life had been full of them, and people I'd cared about were responsible… though it had taken me coming here to the Niche to find out the truth. Just thinking about it made me angry to the core.

Or did the fact that it was done for a good reason—saving all humankind—excuse the deceit?

"Something I don't understand," I said. "Before Mother cut me off, I had the memories of all her avatars. If that's the case, why didn't I remember *any* of this backstory? Why is it all *new* to me?"

"It's hard to say." Maeve shrugged. "Maybe she enabled you to retain only the memories she *wanted* you to have. Maybe she just built you that way, and the Ancestrum didn't detect and override that part of your programming."

I shook my head unhappily. "If I'd known all this, it would have changed everything. My whole *life* would have been different, I *know*."

"Well, we can't go back and change it," said Maeve. "We can only move forward and deal with the trial at hand."

A wave of foreboding washed through me, and I fought to push it away. "So when *is* the trial, anyway? How long do I have to get ready?"

"We were going to wait till tomorrow morning, to give you all some time to rest," said Maeve. "But we've had to speed things up. According to our intel from the outside world, Mother Earth is making her big move sooner than expected."

"So, when will it be?"

"Two hours from now." Maeve shrugged apologetically. "But don't worry, you'll be fine. Just tell the truth and speak from the heart."

"Nothing to worry about then," I said. "It's not like the future of all humanity is riding on this, is it?"

Maeve reached over and touched my arm. "You have a lot of

supporters among the Ancestrum, Gaia. We're on your side…and humanity's side, too. We'll get you through this."

"Thanks, that's good to know." Even as I said it, my mind roiled with doubt and fear. Ever since my life had gone off the rails back in Confluence, nothing had gone the way I'd expected. Every turn had made things a little worse, a little shakier. Expecting the best this time didn't make sense, especially with so much at stake. But how could I live with myself if I failed, and my failure led to humankind's extermination?

My powers were gone, my confidence shot, my closest friends out of reach, and the fate of the human race was in my hands. Could I have possibly faced a bigger challenge with less of an edge?

"I hope this hike has helped, at least a little," said Maeve. "It's good to clear your head, especially after what you've been through."

I gestured at the trail where it continued along the lip of the ravine. "Actually, I think I need to clear it some more…by myself, if that's all right."

Maeve nodded. "Of course, I understand. Just please return to the village in an hour or so to prepare for the trial."

"I will." I smiled. "Don't want the Ancestrum not to hear my side of the story, after all."

"No, you really don't want that." She waved and started back down the trail the way we'd come. "You're the voice of reason, Gaia Charmer. If you can't save humanity, no one can."

I wandered alone for a while after Maeve left me, lost in thought. I kept trying to get ready somehow, to organize some ideas for my testimony at the trial…but my thoughts kept scattering. The pressure and uncertainty were too much.

I truly felt as if I were on my own in this challenge, the weight of the world resting heavily on my shoulders. I alone could hold off Armageddon…though I'd never felt less capable in my entire life.

I found myself wishing I were home with my support system around me. Duke, Luna, Briar, Ashanti, and Nephelae never steered me wrong. I knew they'd have wisdom to offer—even Duke, especially Duke, though he'd apparently kept me in the dark my entire life about my true nature.

But I couldn't imagine reaching out to them was an option in the Niche. Just when I needed them most, the people I knew and trusted best were truly out of reach. All I had to turn to was myself.

And a self who looked just like me, emerging from a copse of trees along the trail in my path.

"Hello, Echo." Gaia 2's smile had a cruel gleam as she stepped in front of me, tossing off a jaunty wave. "Funny meeting you here, don't you think?"

I stopped and tensed, instantly on guard. Even without her powers, I was sure she could be a potent threat—out there especially, alone on the trail.

"'Echo?'" I said.

"It's all you are." She chuckled. "A weak echo of the original war-self, me."

"What do you want?" I glared, bunching my fists at my sides. For the umpteenth time, I instinctively reached out for a link to the world and its power—but of course, I was still cut off.

"Kiss and make up?" She puckered her lips and kissed the air while bobbling her head mockingly from side to side.

I stood my ground, every sense on high alert for the first sign of the attack I guessed was coming. "You should walk away while you still can," I told her, my voice icy. "Just leave."

"But don't you want to know your surprise?" She bounced on the balls of her feet, a silly grin crawling over her features. It was hard getting used to seeing that face, a mirror image of my own, from such a short distance away.

"No." I was ready to fight or run, depending on what she had up her sleeve. "Any surprise you have is of no interest to me whatsoever."

"Wrong again, Echo." Gaia 2 smirked and pointed the index fingers of both hands at me. "*This* one is *mucho* interesting. It is *change-your-life* interesting."

"I don't care. I have nothing to say to you." *Murderer*, I wanted to add. *Monster. Bitch.*

"Then you don't want to know how to fix this whole mess?" She raised her eyebrows. "You don't want to hear how to make this effed-up situation go away?"

I didn't trust her. "Piss off." Squaring my shoulders, I took a step toward her, trying to intimidate her into shutting up and going away.

She just stood there and smirked. "I'll tell you anyway, because I'm such a sweetheart. Because I, at least, am willing to look past our differences and give you another chance."

"*You* want to give *me* another chance?" I snorted. "How generous."

"Why not? We have so much in common, after all." She fanned her hands around her face and wiggled her fingers. "We are literally cut from the same cloth, sweetheart. Does it *look* like we're meant to be on opposite sides?"

I bristled as her words sank in. "We could *never* be on the same side."

"But we *could*," she said. "It's called an *alliance*."

I shook my head, filled with disgust. "With what you've done, and what you're planning to do, I'd never in a million *years* be your ally."

"But you haven't heard the rest of the sales pitch yet," said Gaia 2. "For one thing, if you join Team Mother with me, all your sins will be forgiven. Everything you've done to get in the way of her justice will be forgotten."

I had some choice words ready, but I held them back and listened. Maybe that was the best way to get her to get to the point and leave me alone.

"And that's not all," said Gaia 2. "If you join our little alliance, you will also get to keep a handful of pet humans even after the rest of the species is wiped out. Best of all—*best of all*—you'll get to save a chosen mate with whom to restart the human race!"

I frowned. "Why would Mother restart humanity after going to the trouble of wiping it out?"

"She'll introduce certain—*upgrades*—to make humankind more...*civilized*. More forward-thinking. Less destructive. She's learned a lot about how people *shouldn't* be this last time around."

"I see." I pretended to think it over, though I had no intention of taking her up on her offer. "That's interesting."

"Isn't it?" She grinned. "And I'm *confident* I can sell it to Mother Earth. She'll be so happy to get you on board, she'll accept the terms in a heartbeat."

I just nodded, remembering how awful I'd felt since being cut off from Mother. I could never buy into this bitch's alliance, but part of me certainly wished I could, just to reconnect with Mother Earth.

Even though it was true, since the big separation, I'd learned and experienced so much as an ordinary human that I'd never known or experienced as a tuned-in avatar.

"So, what's the verdict?" asked Gaia 2. "Can I put you down as a yes?"

"If I do, what happens after that? Neither of us has powers here."

"Neither do the Ancestrum women; they're so worried about

drawing Mother's attention." Gaia 2 sneered and nodded. "That's why you and I could make a real splash if we join forces."

"You and I?"

"Just imagine it!" she said. "Even without powers, the two of us could really tear this place apart!"

I had my doubts about that, but I just nodded.

"So, what do you say?" asked Gaia 2. "Yes or no?"

I shrugged. "I appreciate the offer," I said, though I didn't really. "The problem is…"

"Think about it," she said, extending her hands with palms out. "Between now and the trial, give it some thought, then give me a signal."

"But I can already tell you…"

"Did I *mention* the awesome super special bonus?" she asked. "What is perhaps the *greatest* reason for accepting this one-time-only offer?"

I sighed. "What's that?"

"If you *do* accept the offer," said Gaia 2 with her most sinister, reptilian smile yet, "I might not *kill* you."

Then she whirled and ran back into the woods, laughing all the way.

The Ancestrum weren't wasting any time. When I returned to the village after my hike, Maeve rushed me right to a massive amphitheater carved out of a hillside a short distance away. Every stone bench in the place was already packed with women in white garb, hundreds of them talking among themselves as they awaited the proceedings.

"This is it," said Maeve as she led me down the tiers toward the stage. "These women are about to decide the future of humankind."

Looking around as we descended, I met one gaze after another —just as many frowning as smiling. "Why do I get the feeling that future isn't such a sure thing?" I said.

"We don't know how it will shake out yet," said Maeve. "Just do your best."

Across the amphitheater, I saw Gaia 2 walking down the tiers with Tess at her side, approaching the opposite end of the stage. Just as I spotted her, Gaia 2 blew a kiss in my direction, then waved.

That started me thinking about what I'd do to her first if I got my powers back at the trial. Have the ground swallow her up? Crush her with a giant boulder? Bury her in mud and flash-fossilize her?

All of the above sounded good to me.

Just then, Maeve interrupted my daydream. "Look who's here."

We reached the bottom tier, and she gestured at the front row of the audience. Georgia, Mid, Ebon, and White Buffalo all sat there, side by side, and smiled as we approached. Beatrice Brown sat alone at the far end of the row, scowling at Gaia 2's mark on the stage.

"Thanks for coming," I said, then focused in on Ebon. "How are you feeling?"

"Pretty good, considering I almost died," he said. "And rethinking the whole extinction thing that's been my mission in life. Turns out it's not as much fun when *you're* the one going extinct."

I reached for his hand, pressing it between both of my own. "I'm just glad you're here, Ebon. I need all the friends I can get right now."

"Friends." He nodded. "Right. That's us."

Maeve cleared her throat. "Everyone, please remember not to interrupt or intervene unless asked to do so. Gaia must stand on her own to argue the merits of her position."

"Shouldn't she have an *attorney*, at least?" asked Georgia.

Maeve shook her head. "The rules are different here. Lawyers just get in the way, especially when time is short and the stakes are as high as they are now."

"How short is it?" asked White Buffalo. "The time, that is."

"You don't want to know," said Maeve, leading me away by the arm.

She stopped at one of two white rings painted on the gray stone surface near the edge of the stage, ten yards apart. She gestured at the nearest ring, indicating I should step inside, but I hesitated.

"Don't worry," said Maeve. "That's just the mark where you'll stand during the trial. Gaia Grenoble will stand in the one over there." She pointed at the other ring, then turned and gestured at a stone throne in the middle of the stage, some distance back from the rings. "And that is where the arbiter will sit as she conducts the proceedings."

Before I could ask another question, a chime sounded three times in quick succession. The noise from the crowd faded, and everyone in the amphitheater stood.

Gaia 2 just made it to her mark as Drusilla, the first person we'd met after arriving in the Niche, emerged from a doorway in the stone wall along the back of the stage. Her chestnut hair was arranged in an elegant pile atop her head, bound with leafy garlands, and her white shift had been replaced by a black gown tied with golden cords.

It didn't take a genius to guess who the arbiter was.

"Welcome, beloved sisters and honored guests." Her voice, which had been raspy when we'd first met, was strong and clear, not even slightly hoarse. Her tone was commanding, her bearing regal. "We have come here today to render judgment on a matter most grave. At stake is no less than the very survival of the human race itself."

Eyes glinting, she looked around at the hundreds of women in the amphitheater. "We have never before faced a crisis on this level. The Ancestrum has never been so divided. But fate has brought this burden before us, and we accept it as we have always accepted the burdens of service for which we were created."

Everyone remained quiet and fully focused on Drusilla as she spoke—except Gaia 2, who was watching me intently the whole time. When I looked over, annoyed, she sneered and winked in my direction. I ignored her and returned my eyes to Drusilla.

"Two women have come before you to make their pleas," she continued. "They may look the same, but make no mistake—they have very different points of view.

"Please listen and consider the merit of their arguments with care, informed by your own unique experience as avatars. Like me, like them…" She gestured at me and Gaia 2. "…every one of us is both Earth and human, world and flesh. We have the special ability and responsibility to see both sides of this matter in all their complexity and understand them at the deepest level.

"Let us, therefore, clear our minds and hearts, hear the testimony of these two passionate speakers, and find concurrence among us on what is surely the most weighty and consequential decision of our lives."

When she finished, everyone applauded, signaling their approval. I only clapped a little, because my mind was very much elsewhere…wondering what the hell I was going to say when it was my turn.

I hoped I wouldn't go first, because my mind was blank. I knew I should've spent my hiking time coming up with some kind of talking points, but I hadn't. I'd been too distracted by Maeve's flood of information, then Gaia 2's offer of alliance, to sort out what I might say. Was that intentional, I wondered, at least on Gaia 2's part?

Looking over at her sly, confident smirk, I could believe it.

As the applause faded, Drusilla spoke again. "Before we start in earnest, however, I ask that you all join me in a moment of silent meditation for our lost sisters, Ellie Grenoble and Imogene Parker.

"These two great women served as avatars of Mother, as we all have. Instead of retiring here to the Niche, they chose to remain in the world outside, monitoring the avatar, Gaia Charmer, and reporting her activities to us.

"They were killed by Gaia Grenoble as part of Mother's war on humanity, to frame Gaia Charmer for murder and provide a further impediment to her interference in the conflict. But we will not dwell on these dark deeds today, as more pressing matters consume our attention.

"Let us instead remember these two casualties of war and all the good they did with their lives. Let us lift them up with the energy of our own spirits. We will join you soon enough, sisters."

The Ancestrum repeated her last line, and everyone raised their arms in the air, hands cupped toward the sky. A golden nimbus radiated from the audience, pulsing softly like the beating of a heart. The nimbus glowed brighter, reaching a peak that I had to shield my eyes from…and then it gently ebbed, melting back into the gathered women.

Slowly, they lowered their arms.

It had been a beautiful tribute…but I wasn't as moved as I should have been. All I could think was that the bitch who'd killed those two old women was standing ten yards away, looking not the slightest bit repentant. If anything, she looked bored, standing with her arms folded over her chest like a petulant teenager.

Oh, how I wanted to beat the living daylights out of her.

"And now," said Drusilla, "let us proceed with the reason we have all gathered here today. Mother wishes to wipe out humanity, and only the Ancestrum can stand in her way…if we choose.

"Let us, therefore, hear what these two have to say." She

gestured at Gaia 2 and me. "Let us judge the matter based on their testimony, setting aside any acts they may have committed that we might find objectionable."

I guessed she was talking about Gaia 2 murdering Ellie and Imogene, though "objectionable" wasn't the word I would have used to describe what she'd done. How she could instruct the Ancestrum to set aside those acts was beyond me; it made me wonder just how fair and sensible this whole trial was going to be.

"Regarding the rules of order, though no hard limit will be placed on a speaker's time, I reserve the right to end her testimony at my discretion. If the testimony becomes unproductive, misleading, abusive, or overextended to force a certain outcome by delaying action, I will end it. As arbiter, this is my sole right.

"I also reserve the right to call witnesses if I think they will add relevant substance to the testimony and help us to arrive at a consensus.

"And so." Drusilla walked to the stone throne and stood before it. She extended an open hand in Gaia 2's direction, and a wave or relief washed through me. "In deference to her seniority as an avatar, let us begin with the testimony of Gaia Grenoble. Proceed."

With that, she sat on the throne, one hand on a stone-headed gavel on the armrest at her right. Everyone else in the amphitheater sat, except Gaia 2 and me.

Gaia 2 gathered herself up and cleared her throat. Then, the sweetest, most honest smile of all time spread over her face, and she started talking.

"I love Mother Earth." Her voice rang out, perfectly pitched to reach every ear in the amphitheater. "There, I said it.

"I love Mother, and I think…I *know* you all love her, too.

"We can't help it, can we? We were *made* to love her, even after we are separated from her and replaced by the next generation."

I didn't miss the quick look she shot my way when she said that.

"Can we, therefore, turn our backs on Mother in her hour of need?" she continued. "As humanity pushes her—and *themselves*, don't forget—to the brink of destruction, can we stand back and just let it happen?" Her warm smile became a steely glare. "I say we cannot.

"I say we must do everything in our power to preserve our life-sustaining Mother, no matter the cost." Her voice trembled. "And make no mistake, the cost will be high.

"I'm sure I speak for us all when I say we *don't* want to do this. We *shudder* at the thought of extinguishing billions of human lives." She paused, dramatically staring off into space. "It goes against *everything* we believe in.

"But how many of us would be willing to kill *Mother* instead?" Again, a pause. "Because make no mistake, that is *exactly* what we'll be doing if we don't end the human threat in time. We'll be sacrificing Mother Earth, the world-spirit we have dedicated our lives to *protecting*.

"And once she's dead, the humans will die *anyway*. So any attempts to save them are misguided and doomed. Either way, they *die*." Her voice rose, impassioned. "They. Will. *Die*." She pounded a fist in the palm of her hand to punctuate each word.

"So, in that regard, nothing you do will make any difference," said Gaia 2. "You can't stop humankind from perishing. The only thing you *can* change is if they take Mother Earth down *with* them. *That* is your only decision.

"And I know what *I* would do in your shoes. There isn't a doubt in my mind. Because *I* don't want to see the Earth's ecosystem collapse…her climate become inhospitable to all but the most tenacious forms of life…her very *crust* split open from the blasts of nuclear missiles in a final paroxysm of human conflict over dwindling resources. I don't want to see that happen and know I could have done something to stop it.

"That's why I'm asking you to return my powers, return me to Mother Earth, and either join my crusade or stay out of my way as I wage it. That's all I'm asking, and I know you know it's the right thing to do.

"So *do* it!" Gaia 2 pumped her fists in the air, and some of the crowd applauded.

As the applause continued, and Gaia 2 kept pumping her fists and reveling in the attention, Drusilla banged her gavel over the noise. "Ms. Grenoble." She had to raise her voice again to be heard. "Ms. Grenoble! Are you done? Have you finished your testimony?"

Gaia 2 turned and gave her a thumbs-up. "I think that covers it, your honor."

"Very well." Again, Drusilla banged the gavel, and the crowd quieted. "Then that brings us to our second speaker in this proceeding. Gaia Grenoble has presented her view of the matter. Now, it is Gaia Charmer's turn to speak her mind."

My stomach twisted as all eyes turned to me. My tension levels across the board rocketed as I faced what could very well be the most important moment of my life.

Of all the battles I'd fought, wielding great powers against enemies with great or greater powers of their own, I felt least prepared for this one. All I needed to command were words and emotions, but somehow that intimidated me more than a battle royale between superhuman forces.

I felt utterly naked and vulnerable before the Ancestrum, as if I were caught in a nightmare. Panic rose in my tightening chest, making my breaths come quick and short…but then my eyes drifted to the front row of the audience, and I remembered.

I wasn't alone.

Mid, Ebon, Georgia, and White Buffalo all sat there, smiling. Mid nodded encouragingly, Ebon gave me two thumbs-up, and Georgia winked. They were all on my side, believing wholeheartedly in our cause, and they weren't about to desert me.

Even Maeve, whom I'd only just met in the Niche, had a supportive smile on her face. She sat at the end of the front row near me, apart from the others, just as Tess sat at the opposite end nearest Gaia 2…and there was no doubt or disbelief in her expression.

Feeling stronger, I squared my shoulders, straightened my jacket, and pushed aside the panic. I forced myself to take slower, longer breaths, relaxing my chest and belly…and the words started to come.

"Look around you," I said, projecting my voice to fill the amphitheater. "Look at your neighbors. Are they—are *you*—just rock and dirt? Lumps of clay? Globs of mud?

"Of course not! We have heads and arms and legs and hearts and brains. We think and act and speak and feel and sleep. Just like human beings.

"Because the truth is, as avatars, we are just as much *human* as *Earth.*" I spread my arms, displaying my own human form.

"We are not just made to *look* human, to blend in with the human population. We are fashioned from human flesh, with human minds and needs and emotions. We live human *lives*, in human *societies,* and do everything we can to protect our fellow women, children, and men.

"Though sometimes we forget, don't we? Our passion for our Mother and our mission is so strong, it can override the human qualities we cherish.

"At a time like this, especially, it is tempting to put aside our humanity. When we see the terrible things the human race has done and is doing to our beloved Mother, turning our backs on our human heritage might seem like a rational response.

"Why would we want to be associated with those destructive and short-sighted people? Why would we ever want to embrace those monsters who are killing the world that we love with all our hearts?

"But *they* are a part of *us*. The Earth might be our Mother, but they are our brothers, sisters, friends, and lovers. We *know* them as we know ourselves. And we *know* they aren't perfect…but do they deserve to be *annihilated?*

"Think of all the people you have loved." As I said it, I looked at my friends in the front row. "Think of the *good* humans have done. Think of the *beauty* they have created. Consider the amazing things they might yet accomplish if given the chance."

I paused to let the words sink in. Took a deep breath. Let it out slowly. "You know Mother loves them, too. Why else would she have made *us* in their image?

"So perhaps the better thing to do, the *nobler* thing, is to try to *heal* instead of *slaughter.* To have faith in our fellow humans instead of giving up on them.

"Granted, they are on a destructive road. We cannot let them continue the way they have been, or they *will* wipe out both themselves and their Mother. The status quo is no longer enough.

"But I say, instead of falling back on the old ways, instead of wiping out humanity wholesale, we try something *new.* Perhaps, as avatars, we are best equipped for this role, most ready as a melding of Earth and humanity to save them both.

"And that, I say, is what we should do. We should accept our new purpose as unique intermediaries between the world and its people, helping them both to step back from mutual destruction, and instead leap forward into a bold new era of mutual support and sustainability."

I paused for effect, looking around at all the avatars. I swear, they had the best poker faces ever. I couldn't tell from looking at them who was taking my side and who wasn't.

Was anything I said making any difference at all? Until the final tally, all I could do was say what came to mind and hope for the best.

"We all wish we could save the world, don't we?" I said. "And I'll bet we all wish we could save humanity, too.

"I say there's no reason we can't do both. We avatars, with the accumulated power, experience, and wisdom of tens of thousands of years, can *surely* come up with a solution that accomplishes those seemingly impossible goals.

"In so doing, we can forge a world—and a human species—that are stronger, brighter, and longer-lasting than any that have come before. Maybe *that* is why this crisis has come about—to pave the way for a better world and people."

I spread my arms wide to encompass all the avatars and raised my voice for the grand finale. I felt a shiver of excitement as I brought home the last line of my message, hoping to make it memorable and inspiring for the crowd.

"And maybe, just maybe, it's why all of *us* were created in the first place."

I nodded at Drusilla, signaling I was done. Some of the audience members applauded, though I couldn't tell just how many. It seemed there were more than those who'd clapped for Gaia 2, but I wasn't sure.

All I knew was that I was done, for better or worse, and the rest of it was out of my hands now.

Drusilla banged the gavel. "That concludes the testimony!" She banged it again. "The speakers will now leave the amphitheater and await our verdict. It is time for the Ancestrum to discuss and decide the fate of the world and all humankind."

"Geez!" Georgia shook her head with frustration. "What kind of place *is* this where you can't even bribe an *arbiter* with sexual favors to save the human race?"

We all looked at her at once, and she laughed.

"I'm kidding, I'm kidding!" she said. "I would *never* try bribing these ladies with sex! Fashion makeovers, *maybe*." She laughed again. "I mean, seriously—someone's gotta *tell* 'em those white slips they're all wearing aren't *cuttin'* it."

I smiled, glad for the distraction. She, Ebon, Mid, White Buffalo, and I were holed up in a cave behind a waterfall while the Ancestrum figured out their consensus. Gaia 2 and Beatrice were somewhere else, presumably also a soundproofed location.

With the noise from the rushing water, our cave was one of the few places in the Niche where they figured we wouldn't hear what they were saying…those of us without the power of enhanced listening, at least. As for Mid and White Buffalo, they were sworn not to tune in even if they could, since the Ancestrum's debate was supposed to be completely confidential.

"I wasn't paying attention to what they had on," I said, pacing restlessly across the cave and back. "I was just trying so hard to get through to them."

"You did great, hon." Mid, who was perched on a relatively dry rock in the back of the cave, nodded. "You'd have gotten *my* vote—

if I was *allowed* to vote, that is." Though Mid was technically part of the Ancestrum, her sisters had blocked her from voting for being too close to me and therefore not being objective enough. It was the same reason she was stuck in a cave with me instead of sitting in on the discussion in the amphitheater.

"It was an awesome speech, all right," said Ebon, who stood at the rim of the cave and gazed into the falling water beyond. "It totally gave me goosebumps, especially the part about how I'd inspired your impassioned defense of humanity with my amazing human good looks and sex appeal."

I shot him a smirk as I walked past him in my latest round of pacing. "Just glad I could give credit where credit was due."

"So, what's the good word, huh?" Georgia strolled over and leaned against the wall near Mid. "Can you hear through the waterfall? What are they saying back at the thunderdome?"

Mid shrugged. "I don't know."

"You don't *know*, or you can't *tell* us what you know?" asked Georgia.

"They'll tell us when they're ready," said Mid.

Georgia snorted. "Thanks for the awesome service, Miss Ancestrum. You are getting *such* a shitty tip when this is all over."

"I still think you did great, Gaia," said Ebon. "They didn't make it easy for you, either. Drusilla told everyone to *disregard* the war-bitch's two cold-blooded *murders*, for crying out loud!"

"Right after the moment of silent meditation for her victims!" chimed in Georgia. "What bullshit!"

"Drusilla had to give the appearance of objectivity," said Mid. "But by having a moment of remembrance for the victims, she made sure they wouldn't be forgotten."

White Buffalo, who'd been sitting quietly in a corner until now, finally spoke. "So, what happens if they vote against us? Against humanity?"

"I assume they'll power up the war-bitch and turn her loose back home," said Mid. "At which point, she'll link back up with Mother and go to town wiping people out."

"I see." White Buffalo nodded slowly. "And what will *we* do in that case?"

Nobody answered.

"What is our Plan B?" asked White Buffalo.

"We don't have one, do we?" said Georgia. "How *can* we?"

Ebon continue to watch the back of the waterfall, arms folded over his chest. "Assuming they send us home, and they don't restore Gaia's powers, what can we do? How can we possibly stand up to a powered-up war-bitch and Mother Earth?"

"We can't, hon," said Mid. "We'll be better off staying here."

"You *think* so?" asked Georgia.

Mid nodded sadly. "Do you really want to be there to see humanity wiped out?"

"But the rest of us have powers, even if Gaia does not," said White Buffalo. "Maybe all our powers, used together, can at least stop the war-self."

"At which point Mother will destroy us," said Ebon.

"But at least we will die in battle, in defense of all humanity." White Buffalo rose and walked to the middle of the cave. "At least we will perish with *honor* and *courage*, having done all we can to save the people of the world."

Everyone fell silent for a long moment, considering.

"She's not wrong," Georgia said finally. "Surviving would suck anyway. Who wants to live in a world without any damn people?"

"Wait." I marched over to face Mid. "What about our supporters?"

She scowled. "Who?"

"Maeve said we have supporters among the Ancestrum," I said. "That doesn't change if we lose the vote. What if we could get them to help us, even if the trial doesn't go our way?"

"I can't imagine it would ever happen," said Mid. "The Ancestrum always acts in concert. A losing side would never go against the results of a trial."

"There's a first time for everything," I said, though I didn't feel nearly as confident as I sounded. "And the stakes have never been higher, have they? Maybe our sympathizers will say, the world's going to hell anyway, let's throw 'em a bone."

"Or maybe," said Mid, "some of them will rat us out, and the Ancestrum will lock us down hard. They can be plenty brutal when they want to be, honey, trust me."

"Brutal?" asked Georgia. "How brutal?"

"Are you trying to tell us something, Mid?" said Ebon. "Is there something they might do to us if we lose?"

Before Mid could answer, the sound of footsteps crunched on the pathway leading up to our cave. We all looked in that direction just as Maeve entered the cave.

"Hi everyone." She smiled. "The verdict is in."

I stared hard at that smile, looking for any indication of the outcome…but I came up empty. Beyond the polite expression she wore for our benefit, she was playing her cards close to the vest.

"What now?" asked Ebon.

"You come with me back to the amphitheater," said Maeve. "You and Gaia Grenoble will stand before the arbiter and receive your verdict and sentence."

"Which is?" Georgia bugged her eyes, wagged her head, and fluttered her hands.

Maeve just kept that noncommittal smile in place. "You're about to find out." She gestured at the path she'd just ascended. "Now, if you'll please come with me?"

"Wait." I stepped up beside her and turned to the group. "I just want to say, no matter what happens…I appreciate everything you've all done for me. I couldn't have made it this far without you."

"Any time, hon," said Mid.

"You got it, baby!" said Georgia.

"Even if this all goes badly," I continued, "and everything falls apart, I will treasure the memories of fighting the good fight with all of you."

Without a word, White Buffalo stepped forward and took my hand. Then, she hugged me, her willowy, warm body pressed tightly against mine.

The others joined the hug, too, piling on around me…and I smiled. On the verge of a verdict that could end my life as I knew it and end the lives of all humanity…far from my home and the people I'd known and loved for so long…without my powers or any idea what the future might hold…I at least had that moment to savor. To keep me from going through the crucible. To keep me from falling apart when I needed most to keep myself together.

And maybe that, in the end, was all that truly mattered in the world.

29

Back in the amphitheater, back on my mark, I nervously twisted my braid and waited for whatever was coming next.

The crowd was restless, too, talking and shifting on their benches…though I couldn't tell if that was a good thing or a bad one. The women of the Ancestrum were keeping their intentions to themselves.

If only Gaia 2 would do the same. Standing on her own mark, she cleared her throat loudly to get my attention. When I finally looked her way, she pointed an index finger at me, then gave me a thumbs-down as if I'd already lost the trial.

I win. She mouthed the words, overpronouncing to the hilt for my benefit. *You lose.*

There were so many things I wanted to say, so many gestures I could have offered, but I contented myself with ignoring her and turning away. If she *was* the winner here, I wasn't going to make her victory sweeter by showing her she was getting on my nerves.

She cleared her throat again and again, but I didn't look. I was done giving her the satisfaction she so desperately craved.

Finally, the triple chime sounded, indicating the trial had resumed. Everyone in the amphitheater stood, looking solemn.

I heard familiar footsteps behind us then and looked back to see Drusilla approaching through the doorway in the wall at the back of the stage. With all the regal bearing in the world, she glided to the throne and took up her gavel.

"Let us finish this." She banged the gavel hard on the arm of the throne and sat. "We, the Ancestrum, have made our choice.

"Let it be known that we did not make it lightly," she said. "We discussed this matter with all due gravity and considered the concerns of everyone involved.

"In the end, however, we were so divided, a clear-cut mandate was impossible to achieve," continued Drusilla. "Neither side won the majority…not even by a single vote."

My gaze met Gaia 2's, and for once, I could tell we shared the same reaction: surprise and disbelief.

Neither of us had won…or had we?

"We talked some more and voted again…but the result was the same," said Drusilla. "After the third time yielded the same outcome, we realized a tie was the best we could hope for. The Ancestrum is deadlocked.

"Given the nature of this crisis, however, we cannot be content with inaction," said Drusilla. "We cannot fail in our responsibility to resolve this conflict one way or the other.

"Therefore, we have, in a way, made a decision. We made a choice without betraying the intent of our membership.

"This, then, is our verdict." Drusilla rose and walked down to stand between Gaia and her twin. "After considering whether to support Gaia Charmer or Gaia Grenoble—and, therefore, humanity or Mother Earth—we the Ancestrum choose…"

I held my breath, ready to burst from the stress. I didn't know what Gaia 2 was doing, didn't look, didn't care.

"*Both*." Drusilla spread her arms, gesturing at both of us. "We choose *both*."

Both? Gaia 2 mouthed the word with disgust. *How?*

I just shook my head. It didn't make sense to me, either.

"These women, these *champions* of opposing viewpoints, will be given the chance to *settle* this themselves," explained Drusilla. "We will return them to Mother Earth and let them determine the winning solution by fighting it out."

Suddenly, Gaia 2 was grinning, confident she held the winning hand. After all, I had no powers anymore.

But her grin didn't last.

"To ensure they each have the same chance at victory, their power levels will be equalized," said Drusilla. "One will be boosted." She gestured at me. "And the other will be diminished." She gestured at Gaia 2, who was scowling. "To equalize things further, we will ensure each woman has a connection to Mother Earth and all her resources."

Now *that* wasn't equalizing at all. I knew Mother would side with Gaia 2, leaving me at their mercy, even with restored powers.

Drusilla may have anticipated my concern. "In the interest of fairness," she said, "each woman can enlist whatever allies she chooses—though the Ancestrum must of course remain neutral in this regard. These women will not be penalized if others come to their aid."

When I glanced at my people in the front row, Ebon and Georgia both grinned and gave me double thumbs-up signals.

"When one of these women achieves a decisive victory over the other, the Ancestrum will reconsider its verdict," continued Drusilla. "At that time, if so decided, we may restore full power to the winner and also deploy our own combined might in support of her goals... even if it means the fatal exposure of the Niche and its inhabitants.

"That is our decision," she said, lowering her arms to her sides. "And it takes effect *immediately*."

Women approached the stage from the audience, headed our way. Gaia 2 stepped off her mark, looking angry and panicky.

"Wait!" she said. "You can't *diminish* me! I have a *job* to do for Mother!"

But no one seemed to be listening.

"Prepare yourselves!" Drusilla raised her arms overhead. "You're about to fight for what you *believe* in." As she said it, bright bolts of lightning crackled out of her fingertips. Thunder rumbled overhead among the low-hanging clouds.

Suddenly, her lightning lashed out and connected with Gaia 2 and me, stabbing us each in the chest. We both screamed at once, transfixed by the searing heat spiking into our bodies.

There was so much pain, I was barely aware of my feet leaving the stage. Gaia 2 and I rose up in the air, connected through the bolts whipping out of Drusilla's body.

"First, the power transfer!" Drusilla shut her eyes and threw her head back. The lightning surged, and Gaia 2 and I spun, cartwheeling in midair. "We divide it evenly between you. Each of you will have *half* the rightful charge of an avatar."

Slowly, we stopped spinning. If Drusilla was right about me being powered up, I was too dizzy and in too much pain to tell the difference.

"And now, we must send you on your way." As Drusilla said it, a hole opened in the sky, quickly expanding from a pinprick to a portal. A beam of sunlight shot through it and punched down to the stage between us, bleaching the weathered gray stone with its brilliance. It was the first sunlight I'd seen since arriving in the ever-gloomy Niche.

"A word of warning to you both!" said Drusilla, looking up at us. "Be on guard, for the action has already begun, and you will arrive in the middle of it.

"Your friends, who will come after you, will also be deposited in harm's way. There is no place of safety where you are going." Drusilla scowled. "It is literally *Hell on Earth*."

Just as I wondered where she was talking about, I felt myself drifting upward. Gaia 2 was doing the same, though she was twisting and kicking up a storm en route.

"Good luck to you both," Drusilla called after us. "Whichever one of you wins, this is history in the making. *Epic* history!"

"Get her, Gaia!" Georgia shouted from below. "We know you can do it!"

"Humanity's depending on you!" hollered Ebon. "Show 'em what you've got!"

"Saving the world's what you *do*, hon!" said Mid.

"And we will join you in the battle!" shouted White Buffalo. "We will stand by your side in the fire and blood!"

I watched as they all shrank in the distance, tiny figures among the multitude of the Ancestrum in the amphitheater. Gaia 2 and I rose higher and higher, closing in on the portal above.

We were almost there when she flipped the bird at me with both hands, laughing in the sunbeam streaming down.

Then, we were both sucked over the threshold, zipping out of the Niche and back into the world we'd left behind.

30

I am still powerless.

That was what I thought as I plunged from the portal, hurtling toward the ground far below.

I reached out into the world around me, straining to connect with any part of it and save my life—but there was nothing. A vast stretch of green ground spread out below me, scrawled with blue streams, scattered with boulders…and *none* of it answered my call.

I was as cut off as I'd been before going to the Niche, and I was about to die because of it.

A figure dropped into eyeshot then, floating easily to the ground like a falling leaf. It was Gaia 2, and she looked completely unruffled and in control.

"Hi, sweetie!" She had to shout for me to hear her over the rushing wind. "Looks like I won't have to lift a finger to win this shit after all!"

She gave me a fluttery wave, then drew her arms and legs in tight so her body was like an arrow. She angled herself downward and shot away from me, flashing off toward the sun-bathed landscape.

As for me, I continued my uncontrolled plunge.

Again, I reached out with all my might, fishing for some connection, no matter how tenuous. The world still felt utterly dead to me, hopelessly closed off. Either Drusilla had lied about my powers being restored, or something had gone wrong, or…

Time delay.

Without warning, I *came alive* again. My awareness of my surroundings flooded back all at once, filling me with every kind of sensation. It was as if, after too long in absolute silent darkness, someone had switched on all the lights and noise again…and all the smells and tastes and textures as well.

It was so overwhelming, I barely hung on to my focus and thoughts. It was hard enough as it was, with the ground racing toward me.

Seconds before impact, I reached down and threw open a sink-hole in my path. As I dove into it, the hole deepened before me—and dirt sprayed from the sides to cushion my fall.

The deeper I went, the deeper the sinkhole got. The spray of dirt gradually thickened, breaking my fall little by little…until, finally, I came to a stop, face down in the depths of the hole.

And as I lay there, a smile crept over my face, because I could *feel* it all again. Every grain of dirt in that pit was coming through loud and clear, as if it were shouting through a megaphone.

And I could feel the dirt below it, too, and the mud and the clay and…

My smile darted away, replaced by a scowl. Not far away, I could feel something moving with irresistible force, pushing up toward the surface—something massive and powerful and superheated. Probing further, I found other indicators of my location, other characteristic features of the place where I'd landed. I recognized them clearly from my days as the human avatar of Mother Earth, when the world's secrets (most of them, anyway) had been laid bare to me.

I suddenly understood exactly where I was and why Mother and Gaia 2 were starting the extinction of humanity here. It all made perfect sense.

Because the largest supervolcano on the planet had been waiting under Yellowstone National Park in Wyoming, the power and pres-sure in its magma chambers building for untold ages. If Gaia 2 and Mother triggered it, the resulting eruption would blast gases and debris into the sky with terrible force. Its eruption, I knew from my time as Mother's avatar, would also set off a chain reaction that blew the other volcanos in the Ring of Fire that roughly encircled the Pacific Ocean. All those volcanoes erupting at once over such a vast region would turn the atmosphere into a seething bubble that rained down fire and poison on all points of the globe. Before long, all but the tiniest, hardiest life would perish, choking on fumes or buried under ash or melted by showers of blazing hot cinders.

Humankind did not stand a chance against that. I probably didn't either…but I had to try.

Frantically digging around at the bottom of the pit, I widened the shaft and turned myself around so I was facing up instead of down. Then, I started gathering power underfoot, pulling together a charged stream of earth to propel myself out of the hole.

Within moments, I was ready to break loose of the pit. I took a deep breath, about to launch myself up and join the fray.

That was when the walls of the pit suddenly collapsed inward, covering me with dislodged dirt.

Burying me in silent darkness like a corpse.

3 1

Finally, I understood what it meant to have half my power.

If I'd had it all, if I'd been the woman I used to be, I could've burst free of the collapsed sinkhole instantly, with only a thought. Instead, I had to work to part the fallen soil and push myself up through the tube, taking moments to clear a pathway and get myself to the surface.

I came up tired and pissed, emerging like a zombie from a grave. Crawling out on all fours, I spit dirt, cleared my eyes, and heaved in one breath of fresh air after another. Truly, I felt like shit…but I had a job to do.

I pushed up to my knees, determined to get in the game—even as the ground rumbled under me. Looking around the vast meadow where I knelt, I saw the earth buck and ripple like ocean waves, flat land rolling into hills. Pressing my hand on the ground, I felt the cause of it—the magma chambers expanding like balloons, bubbling up on the verge of eruption.

Gaia 2 stood among them, arms outstretched, conducting the volcanic build with a blissful smile on her face. Her powers were limited like mine, but Mother Earth was on her side; I could feel Mother's imprint from a distance, nursing the magma pockets from dormancy into states of excitation, ready to blow.

Stopping her, stopping *them*, seemed like an impossible task…

but I had to try. I wasn't about to let humanity go up in smoke without a fight.

Even if I had to die trying.

Reaching out, I grabbed hold of a nearby rock the size of a fist and hoisted it off the ground, then sent it flying straight toward Gaia 2. She moved at the last instant, but it still winged the side of her head, stunning her.

She staggered and tried to shake it off, but I grabbed another rock, and another, and hurled them at her. One thumped into her gut, making her double over, and the other cracked her left knee. Even as the second one hit her, though, she whipped around and spotted me.

"Bitch!" She flung one of the rocks back at me, then dropped to a crouch and laid her hands on the ground.

I stumbled back, ducking the rock—and felt a telltale tremor in the ground underfoot. I leaped aside and rolled away, just as a geyser of superheated water burst out of the ground where I'd been standing a second ago.

Again, I felt Mother's imprint in that action, ejecting the steaming water from underground. Just as I'd expected, this fight was two against one…and more lopsided even than that, since one of the two siding against me was a planet.

After evading the geyser, I ran a serpentine pattern across the ground between me and Gaia 2—but another fresh geyser nearly caught me, and another after that. Gaia 2, meanwhile, hailed pebbles my way, hitting me more often than not. I responded by flinging a spray of creekbed mud that blanketed her from head to toe.

"I'll kill you!" She pawed at the mud, furious.

That moment, with her guard down, was the perfect opportunity for me. Focusing all my power on the ground underneath her, I tried to open a fresh sinkhole, just as I'd done to save myself from the fall.

It felt as if the ground was going to give…and then it didn't. Resistance from below held it firm, stamped with the unmistakable signature of Mother Earth.

"Damn!" Frustrated, I closed the distance with a final sprint, barreling toward my enemy.

Unfortunately, she cleared enough of the mud from her face to see me coming. Hunching, she threw out a shoulder and met my charge with one of her own.

We collided with shuddering force and toppled to the ground.

Rolling back and forth, we grappled as the earth rumbled and crunched under us. I shot blow after blow through her defenses, and she did the same to me.

"Give up, bitch!" she howled. "Take my offer and join forces with me!"

"I've got a *better* idea!" I told her. "Why don't *you* join forces with *me?*"

Still, neither of us gave in. Bruises and blood erupted as we churned over the grass, acting out our most violent intentions toward each other.

And then, the ground itself erupted as magma pockets burst through from deep underground into the bright light of day.

3 2

Vents of the supervolcano were finally cutting loose, spewing blistering hot lava and smoke in the air. They were far enough away that we weren't instantly scalded into oblivion—but close enough to signal that closer eruptions were coming soon.

Gaia 2 laughed as she landed a solid punch square in the middle of my face. "Here it comes, bitch! The biggest volcanic eruption in hundreds of thousands of years is about to turn the planet into a giant bubble of ash and smoke!"

I responded by sinking a knee deep in her gut and throwing her off as she doubled over in pain. Rolling to my feet, I kicked her hard in the side and did it again, making her flinch and cry out.

Then, I reached out with my powers and brought up bands of hard-packed dirt around her, locking her down. Grunting and squirming, she fought to escape, but the bands kept her planted in place.

Until they didn't. With a burst of Earth-enhanced strength, Gaia 2 broke through the bands, sending lumps of dirt flying. Aiming her own power my way from the tips of her fingers, she turned the ground under my feet into quicksand.

The quicksand dragged me down fast, giving no slack. My first instinct was to grab hold of something, but there was nothing nearby. My second instinct was to work the quicksand with my own powers, transforming it into dust. As soon as the change took hold, I stepped free of where the quicksand pit had been, already sizing up my next attack.

By then, though, Gaia 2 was up and had used her power to grab a plume of lava from one of the vents and fling it right at me.

My mind raced as that searing plume hurtled toward me, hot enough to melt the flesh from my bones. If I were up to full power, I could have flung it aside with ease, but it was coming in too fast, with too much momentum, for my half-powered self to handle.

Instead, I decided to fling *myself*. Reaching down, I found a pocket of hot steam underground and turned it loose, meanwhile carving out a slab of ground under my feet.

The steam burst forth in a geyser, propelling me and the slab up and away from the path of the lava. I came down hard enough behind Gaia 2 to smash the slab to bits, but I wasn't hurt and wasted no time pelting her with the broken bits of slab.

I was just about to drop her in a sinkhole when a massive, jagged fissure raced across the ground toward me, forcing me to leap away to avoid it. I ended up on my ass, tailbone aching from the fall— watching with horror as the fissure quickly widened, and lava bubbled up from the depths of the resulting trench.

Again, I sensed the hand of Mother Earth at work, and again, I realized I could never beat her on my own. I'd known going in that this would be a losing battle, but now the inevitable outcome was smacking me in the face.

"You're dead, bitch!" Gaia 2 perched atop a pillar of earth a dozen feet off the ground, pointing and laughing at me. "You can't even save *yourself*, let alone the *human race!*"

The lava topped the trench and oozed out onto the ground, flowing toward me. As it did, another trench opened on the other side of me, and more lava bulged up and flowed toward me from that direction.

I needed to leap up and get out of there—but when I tried, I was stuck. Looking down, I saw the ground under me had turned to bubbling tar, and it was holding me fast.

Trapped in a tar pit between two lava flows, I realized the contest was about to end…and I wouldn't be the winner.

The harder I tried using my powers to change the tar to dust or sand, the stickier it got. I felt Mother's hand in the mix, resisting my efforts, holding me down for the coup de grâce.

Still, I refused to stop trying. I writhed in the gooey black tar, struggling to break myself free in any way possible—but I couldn't seem to disperse the stuff with a geyser or push myself out with a surge of earth from below or perform any other trick that occurred to me.

Meanwhile, as the lava continued its approach, the heat built from both sides, quickly becoming unbearable. Sweat beaded and ran on my skin, and the superheated air got harder to breathe with each passing second. Heat ripples danced above each flow like waves in the desert air at high noon.

So, this was how I was going to die, I thought. Cooked alive by competing lava flows while stuck in tar…knowing, in the brief moments when I sizzled out of existence, that I had failed miserably in my duties and personal mission. Knowing also that if there was an afterlife, I would soon be joined there by billions of souls slaughtered by the very world that had given birth to them.

As if that weren't bad enough, I had to listen to Gaia 2's bullshit even over the rumbling of the ground and the hissing of the lava.

"Ancestrum!" she shouted from atop her pillar. "I win! Give me my prize! Join me in ending the menace of humanity once and for all!"

The ground shook harder, and more volcanic vents erupted, spewing lava and steam. The sky turned hazy gray with gas and smoke and dust, occluding the sun. Yellowstone was starting to look like ground zero of the apocalypse, its natural beauty defiled by the throes of devastation.

"Ancestrum! I know you can hear me!" howled Gaia 2. "My supposed replacement has *lost*. It's time for you to join the winning side the way you *promised!*"

The Ancestrum didn't answer. No army of avatars rushed in to help Gaia 2 and Mother wipe out humanity. Maybe they were waiting till the bitter end, when the last of my flesh seeped off my bones in the blistering lava.

Cursing, I fought the tar and reached around for some miracle solution, but the only thing that changed was that the air got even hotter. The lava was only a few yards away on either side now, advancing at a steady pace.

With a supreme effort of will, I managed to wrench an arm free —but then Mother slung up a tentacle of tar and dragged it back into the ooze.

I was wearing out fast, and the heat was killing me. With death only moments away, I thought of one last way to escape—in spirit, if not in body. Even at a fifty percent power level, I thought I could send my consciousness into the ley line network. Where I'd go and what I'd do after that, I didn't know, but at least my mind might survive this disaster.

It was surrender, I knew, but there was no other avenue of escape. Maybe, if I could make it down into the network, I could figure something out someday and rebuild myself.

Or not. It might just as well be the last move I'd ever make.

"Ancestrum!" screamed Gaia 2. "Keep your promise! Join me!"

I decided they would be the last words I'd ever hear. I took a deep breath, then another, and steeled myself to take the final leap.

3 4

I was ready to abandon my body, knowing I could never return to it. I'd made peace with taking that step…but I still shivered on the brink of it.

The heat continued to rise as the lava closed in. More vents erupted, spattering the ground nearby with sizzling beads of red-hot molten rock. I had scant seconds left before even the voluntary evacuation of my physical form would not be possible.

Relaxing into the tar, I drew in another deep breath and held it. I was determined to release the spirit from my shell when I let that breath out.

Goodbye. The word echoed in my mind as tears rolled from my eyes. *Goodbye, life.*

Then, just as I was about to breathe out, the ground around me cracked and crumbled. The breath jolted out of me as the bed of tar in which I lay was wrenched upward—but I held the spirit in. One last glimmer of hope flickered to life in my heart, inspiring me to keep it together a moment more.

As I sailed upward, the tar dissolved and fell away, releasing my body. Turning a slow circle, I rose, leaving the blast furnace heat of the lava flows far below me.

Just as I wondered what had happened, White Buffalo glided into sight above me, regal as ever. "Remember me?" she said, smiling.

I nodded, though in the heat of battle, I hadn't given her and the others much thought. I hadn't seen any sign of them and hadn't relied on Drusilla's promise to allow them to help me. Assuming I was completely on my own had been the smart play.

Now here she was, and I couldn't help smiling back at her. "Thank you." If ever there was a goddess worth worshipping, I knew it had to be her.

"Take a breath." Her dark hair streamed around her, and the white fur of her gown fluttered in the wind. "Are you ready to get back in the fight?"

"Yes." I nodded forcefully. "Let's do this thing."

Flipping around for a look at the battlefield, I saw a flock of crows attacking Gaia 2 on her pedestal, knocking her off-balance. Ebon commanded them from the ground with arms outstretched. Further on, Georgia stood in the middle of a stream, sending flumes of water from its bed to drench the raging brushfires kicked up by sparking embers.

But even with their help, I could see the situation was dire. More vents blew open as I watched, tracing the outline of the vast super-volcano. I could feel the massive pool of gas and magma straining underground like a child struggling to be born. It wouldn't be long until all of Yellowstone was consumed, the Ring of Fire went ballistic in a global chain reaction, and the ingredients were set loose to contaminate the planet's atmosphere and kill off humankind.

Armageddon was staring us in the face. We had only one play left to make, if even that would be enough.

"We need to take her down, if we can." I pointed at Gaia 2. "Now that you and the others are here, at least maybe we have a shot."

"She has her own defender, in addition to Mother," said White Buffalo. "But I think Mid can handle her."

She gestured, and I spotted Mid and Beatrice Brown scuffling on the ground in the smoke, the two old women lobbing rocks and dirt at each other the best they could in their much-reduced states.

"All right then." As I watched, Gaia 2 drove off the crows with a volley of pebbles and dirt from her column. "Let's take this bitch down for the count. Shoot me right at her."

White Buffalo slung me headfirst at the enemy. Gaia 2 was too busy batting away the last of the crows to spot me until it was too late.

She cried out as I plowed into her with my fists, knocking her from her perch. The two of us hurtled earthward together, plummeting toward a grassy hill that rippled like a blanket from the tectonic forces driving through it from below.

An agonized cry tore from her lips as she took the brunt of the impact when we crashed down. I pressed the attack from on top of her, punching her again and again in the face.

"I'll kill you!" She thrashed underneath me, trying to toss me away, but I wouldn't budge. "You and all the *rest* of worthless humanity!"

A rock the size of a cinder block flashed toward my head, but I seized control and redirected its flight, casting it into a nearby lava flow. I punched her again, hammering her toward unconsciousness, desperate to win at any cost with the stakes so high.

With one last burst of strength, she flung me off and rolled onto her hands and knees. Bruised and bloody, she clapped the ground with a trembling hand, and a fissure raced toward me like the fuse of a bomb.

The crack widened fast, but I still dodged it and lunged at her, pitching her onto her side in the dirt. She clawed and twisted and kicked, battling like the demon she was, but I wouldn't give her an inch. The earth shook and bucked, but I wouldn't let it throw me.

Then, as the war-bitch launched one more furious blow in my direction, I hauled back both fists and unleashed a heavy strike, sledgehammer-style, at her head.

Finally, her eyes fell shut and she went limp underneath me, out cold.

Now, it was my turn to call out to the Ancestrum, and I did, at the top of my lungs.

"I did it! I beat her!" I cried. "Now it's time to keep your promise!"

Could the avatars in the Niche even hear me over the rumbling quakes and volcanic blasts? If they did, I saw no sign of it—just the ongoing disaster raging all around me.

"Come on! There's no time! If you're going to help me save humanity, you have to do it now!"

Still nothing from the Niche.

It wouldn't be long, I thought, until Mother came after me hard. I had minutes, maybe seconds, until she finally put me down and went on with her business of wiping out the human race.

Soon enough, all the avatars in the world wouldn't be able to save me.

"Please!" I shouted, as loud as I could. "Please keep your word! The people of the world need you! *I* need you!"

Then, my time was up. Instead of an avatar cavalry rushing to my side, a massive fireball leaped out of a volcanic vent and streaked toward me, a cherry red missile engulfed in gold and orange flames.

By the time I saw it, I knew, it was already too late to get out of its way.

I realized two things as the fireball cruised toward me: it was a gift from Mother Earth, and it had been coming for me all of my life.

From the moment of my creation, it had been heading my way. Sooner or later, with a volatile bitch for a mother like mine, it was going to get me. Without becoming the kind of monster she wanted, I could not possibly have avoided it.

Now, there it was, my reckoning for a life well-spent.

As it hurtled toward me, the breath caught in my throat. I only had time to resign myself, not to prepare, as the brilliant glow of the flames held me transfixed. My only regret was that humankind would follow me into death not long after.

Then, suddenly, I was plucked from the ground and hauled skyward, shooting out of the blazing orb's path. Gaia 2 was yanked up, also, and dragged high, her body limp as a rag doll.

Rising and rolling through the air, I saw an incredible vision: rank after rank of avatars, hundreds of them, pouring out of a portal in the sky. They glowed with brilliant energy, shimmering in the smoky haze like angels over the battlefield.

At the head of the group, Drusilla smiled grimly in my direction. "We have come as we said we would." Though the air roared with noise, I could still somehow hear her voice clearly. "We will keep up our side of the bargain as promised."

She clapped her hands, and bolts of lightning burst to life between me and Gaia 2, binding us together. Our bodies jolted and spasmed from the current, and I lost consciousness—then regained it as power surged into me, thrusting me onto another level of strength and awareness.

By the time Drusilla clapped again, cutting off the fireworks, I felt stronger than I had since my jail cell back in Confluence. Stronger even than I'd felt for weeks before that, truth be told; Mother and Gaia 2 must have been sapping my strength for longer than I'd thought.

"You have been restored to full power, Gaia Charmer." Drusilla gestured at Gaia Grenoble as she floated nearby, her body steaming. "As for that one, she has been fully drained. She is no longer a threat to you."

"Thank you," I said. "Just please keep her safe." If I survived this mess—if *humanity* survived it—I would need her to beat the murder rap back home and stay out of prison.

"You now have your own full power, plus the support of the entire Ancestrum," said Drusilla. "Millennia's worth of avatar might, experience, and wisdom at your command. All you have to do…" She bowed her head and spread her arms. "…is command it. What would you have us do, Gaia Charmer?"

With my new army arrayed behind me, I surveyed the battle-field. As I watched, fresh vents exploded, blowing ash and steam and molten rock in every direction. Fresh fissures cracked the ground, and lava flows oozed out of them. The rumbling from underground intensified by the minute, suggesting it wouldn't be long until the biggest blow of all, the one that triggered the whole damn Ring of Fire.

Where the hell should we begin? Time was running out, and there were too many flare-ups to deal with at once.

The more I thought about it, the more it seemed to me there was only one way to end this in the short time we had left.

"We need to take the fight directly to *her*," I told Drusilla. "It's our only chance."

"Mother, you mean?" She frowned.

I nodded. "Go right to the source. Stop her from following through with this, whatever it takes."

"If you mean stop her physically, I don't think that's possible," said Drusilla. "If you mean talk her out of it, I don't think she's feeling very reasonable right now."

"I don't mean either one," I said.

"Something different?" said Drusilla. "Like what?

Just then, another vent disgorged a load of gas and dust not far from where we drifted, adding to the clouds of murk in the air. A moment later, a familiar figure emerged from the murk and soared toward us—White Buffalo, her once-pristine gown soiled with ash.

"Good to see you're in one piece, Gaia," she said. "And the Ancestrum has decided to join us."

"We were just talking about stopping the carnage by taking the fight to the enemy…but I can't do it alone."

"You need a contingent?" asked Drusilla.

Maeve, who'd been listening nearby, waved her hand excitedly. "I volunteer! And I can put together a crack team to go with us!"

I shook my head. "Thanks, but I don't need a team."

Maeve frowned. "But you just said you can't do it alone."

"Correct," I said. "I don't need *some* of you. I need *all* of you."

"All of us?" said Maeve.

"Every last damn one of you," I told her. "Because I think that's what it's going to take."

"To do what, exactly?" asked White Buffalo.

"To stop her," I said. "Once and for all."

36

The sky was full of floating bodies, held aloft by wind currents and clouds of thick vapor generated by White Buffalo and Georgia. It was the only way this could work. If we lay our bodies down on the ground, they'd be vulnerable to attack the instant we sent our spirit selves into the ley line network. None of us would have a physical form to return to when our mission was done.

Even so, we knew we were all still taking a chance. We were high enough the current eruptions couldn't reach us, but if the whole supervolcano blew, it could be a different story. Not to mention, Mother might have a surprise up her sleeve that could bring us all down to Earth…though it was true, if things went well for us, she might be too distracted to play her hand.

Looking around, I saw that most of the Ancestrum had already left. Their bodies hung limp in the sky, arms and legs and hair and white shifts dangling, faces to the sun.

"Okay, then." I'd wanted to be among the last to go so I could be sure everything was working as planned. "Looks like it's about that time."

"It sure does," said Maeve, smiling beside me. "Ready?"

Looking around, I saw White Buffalo hovering nearby, deeply focused with arms outstretched. Georgia sat on a pedestal of ice she'd raised from a stream and frozen with her power, working her fingers in intricate gestures as she kept the vapor clouds in balance under their cargos.

On another pedestal, this one formed from earth, Ebon stood tall and waved his arms overhead, drawing in flocks of birds and swarms of bugs to surround and protect the floating bodies.

The situation was as under control as it would ever be…but I didn't think it would stay that way for long. The amount of effort it took to keep all those bodies aloft and keep them safe just couldn't be sustained forever.

Time, I knew, was truly of the essence.

"Good luck." I reached for Maeve's hand and gave it a squeeze.

"Good luck to us all," she said.

"Let's go."

With that, I leaped out of my body, propelling my spirit self toward the ground below. It was something I'd been afraid to do at half-power, just in case something went wrong…but at full charge, I took the leap without hesitation.

The ground raced toward me, and then I was under it, diving through loamy darkness. For a moment, I became disoriented, uncertain which way was up and which was down. A flicker of panic darted through me as I wondered if I'd somehow gotten turned around and lost.

Then, a constellation of lights appeared in the distance below me, winking like stars in a night sky. There were hundreds of them, twinkling in the darkness.

As I got closer, I heard their voices in my mind, and I knew who they were: the souls of the Ancestrum, waiting for me to join them.

I plunged through their midst and kept going, descending. Their starlight pinpricks swirled in my wake and dove after me in their hundreds, keeping up.

Further down, I spotted what looked like a cord of glowing golden light that marched into the distance as far as I could see. I knew it well, as I'd traveled its kind all over the world, riding from one to the other like a hobo riding the rails.

It was a conduit in the ley line network and as good a starting point as any. Beckoning for the others to follow, I touched it with the spark of my spirit self, and it *seized* me. The next thing I knew, I was rocketing along its length at a furious speed, blazing into the darkness.

Looking back, I saw the multitude of sparks of the Ancestrum holding tight to the conduit behind me, speeding along after me. They followed every time I switched to a new line in the network, smoothly jumping from one rail to another.

Every move took us deeper, closer to the core. Guided by the increasing pressure and heat in the bowels of the Earth, I kept us on track, homing in on our destination.

The closer we got, the stronger the pull of that target became. The massive mind and power of Mother herself drew us in like iron filings toward a magnet, like comets toward the sun.

Even from a distance, I felt dwarfed and had my doubts. How could we succeed against someone like *her?* Could even the assembled souls of hundreds of earthly avatars from throughout history hope to make the *slightest* dent?

Within seconds, those questions were moot.

I shot through a wall of incredibly dense matter and into a vast sphere seething with red light. The Ancestrum stayed behind to await my signal, as we'd agreed before leaving the surface.

At the heart of the sphere, an enormous ball of orange fire churned and flared, throwing off bolts of energy and roaring like the biggest never-ending explosion of all time.

Instantly, I knew where I was. Though I had never been there before, I'd been aware of it all my life—at least until I'd had my powers taken away. It had always waited at the edge of my awareness, its influence felt in a multitude of ways, its power fueling my own.

Of course I recognized it—recognized *her*. That ball of fire and fury spinning in the sphere, ringed with blistering hot magma and blazing with red light, could only be the singular force at the core of my existence…the existence of *all* people and creatures in the world.

Daughter.

Her voice in my head was as familiar to me as her presence.

Traitorous bitch daughter. You have failed me for the last time.

There had been a time when I'd known and loved that voice as well as any voice in my life. Hearing it now, saying such terrible things, made me feel sick. Made me want to run.

But for the sake of every man, woman, and child on the face of the Earth, that was the one thing I couldn't do.

It was time to face up to her and end the battle between us.

Hello, Mother. Good to see you, too.

37

Though I was born into the world as a full-grown adult, there were still times when I longed for a traditional family. Maybe I'd see a child out to dinner with her mother and father, or walking down the street, and I'd feel a sharp pang—a hunger for the love and companionship a family can bring to your life.

But all I'd ever known was the distant presence of Mother Earth, my maker. As much as I'd wished otherwise, I'd only ever experienced that intimate yet impersonal connection—nothing at all like a human mother I could touch and hold and laugh with and love.

Yet I'd still tried convincing myself there was some kind of loving bond between us. I'd still imagined our link was not only as good as that between human mother and daughter, but *better*, in ways other people could never understand.

So, yes, you could say it was a letdown to finally come face to face with her and have her treat me the way she did.

You sick little bitch. Her fiery globe spun faster as she blasted my mind with her nastiness. *I should never have made you.*

Maybe that's true, I said. *But here I am anyway.*

Fucking bitch! The hits just kept on coming. *You can't even defend me, can you? You'd rather side with those miserable human pieces of shit.*

Of course I want to defend you, I said. *I just don't think you need to wipe out the entire human race to do it.*

Mother flared bright, and her magma rings spun into a frenzy. *It is not for you to question my will!*

As she flared and spun, she expanded, swelling to occupy more of the space in the sphere. Even without a physical body, I could feel the heat and pressure increase around me. It was then I knew for sure that she could hurt my spirit form.

But could she kill me in that form? Crush my light out like a firefly underfoot? I had to assume, as my creator, that she could do pretty much anything she wanted to me.

Mother, I've come to talk. It took some effort to push down my fear and stay where I was, but I had to assume time was running out back in Yellowstone and all around the Ring of Fire. *Will you consider sparing humankind?*

Her angry laugh came through loud and clear. *Not a chance. It's them or me.*

She wasn't entirely wrong about that…but I had to say my piece. *What if we could keep them in check? Get them–force them–to stop abusing you?*

Again with the anger-soaked laugh. *How many times have I said the same thing?*

But I could be your enforcer, I said. *I swear, I'll do whatever it takes.*

You've already failed at that job! snapped Mother. *You've already proven you can't do it, you worthless piece of shit!*

She kept expanding, and I backed away. Soon enough, she would engulf me, which I guessed was the whole idea.

This time will be different, Mother, I told her. *I know I've been lax in the past, but this time I'll bring the hammer down. Every time they hurt you, I'll tear them a new one.*

Don't make promises you can't keep. I know you'll never have the courage to do what it takes to stop those people.

Give me one more chance, I said. *What do you have to lose?*

Do you know how many chances I've given humanity? Too many to count! And they've blown it every time. Polluting and destroying is the only way they know how to live.

But what if they know you're a living, thinking being? I asked. *What if we teach them your true nature, and that of Landkind and Waterkind? What if we speak to all of them, not just a few?*

You already know the answer, she said, darkly. *You already know it will only make things worse and speed things up. If those people discover a power in someone else's possession, they won't leave it there for long.*

But, Mother...

Shut up! There's only one way to handle these humans. And there's only one way to handle anyone who opposes it.

Her orange light flared brighter and expanded, pressing toward me. Even in my spirit form, I could feel the heat of her coming closer.

Then, her body roiled and convulsed, changing color. The massive orb of orange fire became a black orb with white highlights, like a negative exposure of the sun. It slid straight toward me, rotating slowly.

The core of Mother Earth was no longer recognizable to me.

I should have done this long ago, said Mother. *Mistakes like you don't deserve to live.*

Suddenly, the black orb shot out an ebon beam that flashed toward me. I moved, but the beam still buzzed my disembodied form—and when it did, a terrible bolt of pain stabbed through me, sending me reeling.

It took a moment to regain my senses, just in time for another blast from the orb. This time, it barely nicked me, but that was enough for more of the same agony as before. It left me feeling utterly drained and scattered, as if another hit or two might blow me apart for good.

I should've expected it, I realized. Of course she had ways of putting down her own creation. She *had* to.

Didn't like that, did you? Her hot magma rings spun faster as she laughed. *Well, tough shit, little bitch.*

Enough, I said. *Please, we can work together and stop humanity without inflicting wholesale slaughter on them all.*

Would you just please shut the hell up? Can't you see I'm busy trying to save my own life, since my good-for-nothing daughter isn't willing to do it?

As I ducked the next two bolts from the black orb, I reached out mentally beyond the core sphere and called for the Ancestrum to join me—but I got no answer, and none of them passed through the wall.

The next beam struck me dead on, hurting like hell as it cooked its way through my mind. When the effect dispersed, I called the Ancestrum again, with the same result as before.

Something had happened to the army of avatars I'd brought along. It was starting to look like I was alone in my fight against the essence of the planet that had made me.

And as yet another blast poured toward me from the black orb, I realized that fight might not last long at all.

38

Die! howled Mother, her black mass billowing closer still.

Her next blast came close, but I dodged it at the last second, pulling my wounded spirit form out of the way. Again, I called for the Ancestrum, and again, there was no response.

Mother, please! I cried, but that didn't stop her from slinging out another bolt. It only nicked me, but the pain was fierce.

I thought of running, but what good would it do me? She was the *world*; she'd catch up to me sooner or later.

And then who would stop her campaign against humankind? Who could stop her from finishing the apocalypse she'd started?

Clearly, it was all down to me.

But how the hell could I stop that out-of-control world-core? Especially now that she'd somehow been corrupted, her very soul blackened with rot.

Bitch! She flung another bolt, which missed. *Worthless bitch!*

My earth-manipulation powers wouldn't do any good against the soul of the Earth herself. I couldn't talk her out of it, either; she wouldn't listen to reason.

There was nothing I had that she couldn't counter or ignore. I was an insect compared to her.

Some war-self you turned out to be! Her voice was shrill with rage in my mind. *You're nothing but a chickenshit do-gooder!* She threw another bolt, and it barely missed me.

Just then, I froze. Something she'd said had gotten through to me.

In her cruel ranting, she'd given me an idea.

There was one thing I had that she didn't have, after all. And that one thing could be just the weapon that a bug like me could put to use.

3 9

The dark star of Mother puffed up even more, occupying almost all of the chamber. Luckily, there was still just enough room for me to get a running start.

You're dead! she shouted, hurling more bolts. *There's nowhere left in the world for you to run!*

I faced her with my back against the wall. Two of the bolts grazed me, but I steeled myself against the pain. No matter what, I had to get through that one last gauntlet.

You're wrong, I told her, gathering my strength. *There is* one *place left for me to go.*

With that, I pushed off from the wall, focusing my spirit self into a long, pointed projectile like an arrow. I sent myself flashing straight toward her, point-first, racing at her seething black center as if a bullseye were painted there.

Stop! she roared, but it was too late. I was already piercing her outer layers, punching deep into her blistering black form.

If I was a bug compared to her, so be it—but this bug had a sting.

Nooo! Her voice was louder than ever in my mind. *Get out!*

I ignored her as I penetrated her deeper layers, leaping closer to her core. It was hard to focus on anything other than my journey, as the forces within her kept trying to slow me down and tear me apart.

The gravity within her grabbed me like phantom fingers, straining to hold me in the darkness until I lost all forward thrust. My momentum pulled me through, but I didn't know how long it would keep me flying.

Though maybe it wouldn't matter in the end. Her contaminated substance was so foul, even to my intangible spirit self, I thought it might kill me before I got where I was going.

I'd hoped my own nature, so opposite her own (a *do-gooder*, she'd called me) might overcome the poison within her. Not only wasn't it working, but her darkness was eating away at me. Whatever Mother was made of now, it was as rancid and corrosive as a lake so polluted, it can no longer sustain life.

I felt terribly sick and tired, like I wasn't going to make it. Slowing to a crawl, I wobbled off course, nearly frozen in my tracks —and then I saw it.

A tiny red light blinking in the distance.

With every bit of will I had left, I managed to push myself onward, ever deeper. The red light grew larger as I approached it, a blinking beacon in the black.

I said get out! Her voice echoed in my mind. ***Get out now!***

As I got closer to the red light, I could see it was a giant gem, a ruby diadem flashing in the night. Shivering from the waves of poisonous corruption through which I passed, I reached for it.

Though I didn't truly know what it was, I longed to touch it. I felt it calling me, drawing me on through the mire.

And then I heard a voice from it, so much kinder and more familiar than the voice that had been blaring out of Mother lately.

Free me. It was a woman's voice, warm and weak. *Free me, lovely daughter.*

It was the true voice of Mother, the one I'd always known.

4 0

<hr>

other?

M   Almost out of momentum, I drifted toward the red gemstone, my reaching spirit-self hands a very short distance away from it. I didn't know what it was, couldn't judge its true purpose, but the true voice of Mother was coming from it, drawing me onward.

My darling, darling girl, she said. *I'm so sorry for everything she's put you through.*

She? I asked.

The new me, said the voice. *My own terrible war-self.*

I stretched toward the gem, nearly making contact. *But Gaia Grenoble and I are your war-selves, aren't we?*

You are my war-selves in human *form,* said True Mother. *The Dark Star is the war-self of the actual planet. The face I wear when the end is near and I must bring out the worst in myself to survive.*

A ripple of shadow-stuff nudged me back a little further from the gem. I stretched out my spirit-form as far as I could and almost covered the distance.

But what good is survival if it means the end of all the people you've raised and nurtured? I asked. *Surely, you can't think it's a good idea to wipe out humanity.*

Of course not, said True Mother. *That's why Dark Star had to take over. Because it seemed the only way to save myself was to end mankind, but I could never bring myself to do it.*

And now you regret it?

It was the biggest mistake I've ever made, said True Mother. *And it's too late to undo it.*

The sadness in her voice was palpable. I wished I could comfort her somehow, to help her feel better—but I had to stay focused on my mission. If humanity hadn't already been wiped out, it would be soon, unless I could do something about it.

What about shutting off Dark Star and taking control again? I asked. *Isn't that something you could do?*

Not anymore, said True Mother. *She's too strong. She had to be. And I'm...I'm too weak now. The humans have done so much damage over the years. I couldn't take back control if I wanted to.*

I nodded, processing what she'd told me. *What about somebody else? Could someone other than you take control?*

True Mother fell silent, as if considering my words. The darkness shifted around me like the waters of a black sea, nudging me closer, then further away, from the ruby gemstone.

Who? she asked. *Were you thinking of someone in particular?*

Maybe. I did the closest thing to a shrug that I could in my spirit form without physical shoulders. *If it's possible, is it something you would support?*

God, yes. I'd give this up in a heartbeat. I've had enough, and the end is in sight. Her heavy sigh echoed in my mind. *Your sister war-self got that much right. Humankind is racing to ruin me, and the clock is ticking.*

As she spoke, I got an idea. If it worked, it would give her freedom, solve my problem, and grant humanity a new lease on life. It would change the world in a fundamental way, and maybe it would save it, too.

What would you need to do to make the transition? I asked.

So you do *have someone in mind,* said True Mother. *Is it you?*

Let's just say it's someone with experience serving and protecting the Earth, I said.

If it is *you, that would be wonderful. There aren't many people who could handle this kind of power, but you've already had a taste of it.*

I think we should try it, I told her. *Humankind is running out of time up there in the world.*

Again, she fell silent for a long moment. *It would be for the best,* she said finally. *I know that. I never imagined it would come to this...but yes.*

You told me you wanted me to free you, I said. *Maybe, given the stakes, it's the right time to step down.*

Though I couldn't see her, I got the impression she was nodding. *I'm not strong enough anymore to fight her,* she said. *Even if I could take control on my own, I couldn't fend her off forever.*

You sound ready to me, Mother, I told her.

So do you, she said. *And I feel better knowing you're the one who'll take the reins.*

I smiled. *I was thinking of someone else, actually. Lots of someones.*

I could tell she was surprised and confused. *Who?*

Dark Star put up some kind of barrier outside the core, I said. *Are you still strong enough to take it down?*

Maybe, said True Mother. *I mean yes, I think so.*

Then do it, I told her, *and you'll see who I have in mind.*

With that, my spirit hands finally landed on the red gemstone, and I finally made full contact with True Mother's essence. I felt her joyful embrace, sensed her power emanating outward in all directions to peel away the shield around the core.

And then I experienced her proud recognition as the Ancestrum poured in—her truest children leaping into the heart of the world to change it forever.

Roaring with rage, Dark Star lashed out with a flurry of furious strikes, blasting the Ancestrum with bolts of searing black energy. I watched through True Mother's eyes as dozens of avatars reeled under the assault, their spirit-forms infused with waves of agony.

But Dark Star couldn't handle hundreds of enemies at once, attacking from all directions. For every soldier of the Ancestrum who was hurt, a dozen more punched through the barrage to pound the black orb with blasts of their own, beam after beam of sizzling power channeled directly from the ley line network itself.

And yet, it wasn't enough.

My children, said True Mother. *Such warriors! Yet they need my help.* Our *help.*

Then let's do it, I told her. *Whatever it takes.*

Dark Star unleashed a frenzied storm of retaliation, blanketing the core in a hail of projectiles forged from her own black substance. The projectiles punched through almost every avatar at once, filling them with pain-inducing current and leaving them scattered and vulnerable.

It was then that True Mother started fighting her from within, using every bit of power at her command and supplemented by my own reserves.

Bitches! howled Dark Star as she reached inward to expunge the threat, burn it out at the root…but that only damaged her own insides. The more she dug after us, the worse it got, as she tore at herself in a desperate attempt to excavate our threat.

But as the Ancestrum rose up again to attack from the outside, Dark Star faltered. Fighting a two-front war wore her down, shrinking her fiery substance as the sustained assaults continued.

Enough! True Mother gathered herself up, the ruby of her soul flashing with renewed intensity. *This ends now!*

True Mother had been locked away for a long time, disconnected and bound in darkness. She was weaker than she had ever been, diminished and broken.

But she still had the force of will to unload one last burst of worldly power.

No more! howled True Mother as a surge of blinding radiance erupted from the ruby. *No more!*

Holding on to the stone for dear life, I heard what sounded like a clap of thunder, and Dark Star convulsed. She cried out in pain, shuddering so fiercely it was as if she was on the verge of exploding from within.

Then, she fell still and silent. I felt True Mother slump within the ruby gemstone, exhausted and depleted.

Mother, I said. *You did it. You stopped her.*

Yes…child. She sounded weaker than ever. *At a cost.*

She was mortally wounded, I could feel it. Her life-force was draining around us. Time was running out.

I'm so sorry, Mother, I told her. *Do you still have the strength to finish what we talked about? To transfer control of the world to the Ancestrum, your children?*

I felt her nod and smile weakly. *Are you certain…you don't wish…to take on the mantle yourself? It would…suit you.*

That means more to me than you'll ever know. Her words moved me. If I'd been in my physical body at that moment, I know I would've cried. *But no, thank you. My purpose lies elsewhere. I can see that now.*

What other purpose…could possibly match this? What calling…could be greater…than running the world?

Saving it, I told her. *Finally living up to the example you set for me.*

You've already…done that, dear. I felt her essence wrap around me;

it was as close to a hug as two disembodied spirit-forms could come. *You've done* exactly...*what I hoped...you would do.*

But I haven't saved you, I said. *I chose humanity over the world. And now you're...now you're...*

Complete. Her voice was growing fainter by the moment. After billions of years at the core of a magnificently elaborate and beautiful planet soaring through space, swimming through the firmament by the light of the sun, she was fading.

The thought of it made me heartsick, especially now that I knew how Dark Star had locked her away and made my life awful in her place. I hated that I'd lost time with her, hating and fearing instead of loving her.

And now, her time was up.

This is how it was meant to be. She gave me one last squeeze, then pushed me away. *Out with the old.*

Suddenly, she blazed with golden, pulsing energy that intensified with each passing second. It built and built, engulfing her in a field of blinding light.

I wanted to be there with her, but I kept backing away instead. I couldn't bear the light and heat she was putting off, the waves of force that were tossing me like a dinghy on the sea.

At last, the biggest wave yet crashed toward me, and I couldn't escape. It flung me away at breakneck speed, sending me rocketing through the layers of True Mother's central orb before I could even say goodbye or thank you.

Just before I shot out of her outermost layer, just before her power exploded in all directions, I heard one thought from her in my mind. Just before the golden rays of her gift intersected with the hundreds of avatars assembled in the sphere, changing them forever, she sent four last words just for me.

Just before the newly empowered and enabled Ancestrum swirled in a celebration of their change, taking up the torch she had passed them with joy and reverence, True Mother gave me one final message to carry with me for the rest of my days.

In with the new. That's what she said, as the avatars became the creator, each with her own bright spirit and style and point of view. As hundreds of gleaming, golden spirits who'd been off the stage for years or centuries or millennia suddenly burst back into the spotlight, revived and ready to put their own stamp on the world-running business.

And then she winked out of existence, her own special spark going dark for all time. It was the first time I'd seen the world end… and then, begin again.

And I finally did shed a tear, or as close as I could come in my bodiless spirit-form.

In with the new.

EPILOGUE

T*wo weeks later...*

"What do you mean, 'no?'" The balding, middle-aged man in the rumpled gray suit and black tie scowled at me, his face turning beet red. "You're a *private eye.* Catching cheating spouses is what you *do.*"

"Not anymore." Tilting back in my chair with my red-sneakered feet on the desk at Charmer Investigations in Confluence, Pennsylvania, I shook my head. "We only handle one kind of business these days, and it has nothing to do with unfaithful partners."

"Then what the hell *do* you people handle?" he snapped.

"Eco-crime," I told him. "Come back when you have a case involving pollution."

He stood there and fumed for a moment, then stormed out, giving the door a hard slam behind him. Luna flipped the bird in his wake, and Duke chuckled.

It was good to be home.

"How long till we get the new sign?" I asked, reaching for my coffee cup on the desk. "So guys like him stop coming around?"

"Should be up in a few days, Earth Angel," said Duke. "After which, we will be clearly identified as Charmer *Eco*-Investigations to all potential clientele."

"And Cruel World *Ecotourism*, of course," added Luna. "Let the rebranding commence!"

I smiled as I sipped my coffee. The changes were part of a shakeup that had been a long time coming. With the Earth on borrowed time, I'd committed myself to fending off the apocalypse by fighting humanity's reckless polluting and ruination of the environment. It was a mission fully endorsed by the Earth Mothers, the planet's new guardian body formed by avatars of the Ancestrum. Powered up and put in charge of the planet and its climate by the late, great True Mother, they were happy with any help they could get in policing the tough new standards needed to save it.

"What about the business cards and social media?" I asked.

"The cards are on order, due next week." Luna tapped keys on the laptop at her desk, checked the screen, and nodded. "And all social media have been updated. Because why?" She smirked in my direction. "Because why?"

"Because sister power!" I shook a fist in the air.

"Damn right." Luna smacked a hand down hard on her desk. "Vitamin S."

"And moon power in general." I raised my cup to Duke, who was leaning on the next desk over. "Great job repairing the office after fake Gaia's rampage while I was gone."

"Nothing to it, Earth Angel," Duke said smoothly. "It was easy as pie, once I got the old band together again."

He meant it literally. He was talking about a big band he'd organized called the Strayhorns, who'd come in and helped with repairs at his behest. If there was one thing the golem with the soul of Duke Ellington was good at, it was leading a band.

"You do know this doesn't change my mind about the world tour, though, right?" I sipped my coffee. "I still can't have you coming out to the general public as you-know-who."

Duke smiled his sweetest, most ingratiating smile, the smile that had launched a thousand concerts during his life. "The thought hadn't even begun to consider the slightest possibility of perhaps at some point crossing my mind, Earth Angel."

He had a way of making me laugh, and he did it again. I'd been through hell, my life had changed so much, but I sat there and laughed like I didn't have a care in the world.

Though it was true, some things were still just getting back to normal.

The bell on the front door jingled, and Sheriff Dale Briar walked in, looking unsure of himself. I couldn't blame him; things hadn't been the same between us since I'd gotten back to town.

"Hello, everyone." He closed the door behind him and took off his hat. "I have some good news. All charges against you have been dropped, Gaia. You are finally, fully in the clear."

A wave of great relief washed through me as his words sank in. Though I'd been back for a week and a half, and Gaia Grenoble (powerless, thanks to the Earth Mothers' intervention) had been in police custody that whole time (delivered from the West Coast thanks to Mid and Ebon), the charges had still hung over me, casting a shadow I couldn't ignore. It had taken a while for the legal system to process Gaia Grenoble, verify my story and the witness statement from the reluctant Beatrice Brown (also depowered by the Ancestrum and brought in by Mid and Ebon), and put the whole frame-up to rest…but I guessed it had finally been resolved.

"That's the best news I've heard all day." I swung my feet down off the desk and stood but didn't approach him. "Thanks for taking the time to stop by and deliver it."

He looked down and shifted his feet. "It was the least I could do, after what I put you through."

"Briar." I walked around the desk to face him. "Nobody thinks any of that was your fault. We all know you only did what you had to, and you gave me a fighting chance when you could."

He shook his head, eyes still cast down. "I should've done more. The hell with the job."

"Hey, no." I started to reach for him, then stopped and reached up to twist my braid instead. "Nothing you could've done would've changed anything. I was going to get caught up in this one way or another."

Finally, his gaze met mine, and I saw the raw emotion within it —sadness, anger, confusion, desperation, hope. I wished I could make it all better, replace it with happiness, but I couldn't, not yet. The feelings I'd had for him had faded to the point of nonexistence. I'd tried so hard to breathe new life into them and failed.

We stood there for a long moment, daring each other to say the next thing. I almost spoke once, then twice, but let it pass. How could I smooth things over or offer any kind of apology or explanation if I didn't even understand myself exactly why things had changed?

In the end, it was Briar who broke the silence.

"For the record," he said, his gaze never leaving mine, "I never, for one second, did not believe in you."

"Thanks." That was all I could think to say in return.

And then, he was gone, marching out the door without a goodbye or backward glance.

Only then did Luna clear her throat. "Somebody get me a sweater. It is *chilly* in here all of a sudden."

I shot her a look, and she returned her full attention to the screen of her laptop. The situation with Briar was one thing I wasn't in the mood to talk about. How could I, if I didn't even understand it myself?

And then there was the *other* situation I couldn't get my head around.

"By the way, Ebon James called," said Luna. "Reminding you of your three o'clock with the 'Earth Mamasitas,' as he called them."

"Shit." My heart starting pounding. "What time is it now?"

"Ten till three," Luna said calmly, as it were closer to five till two. "Correction, nine till three."

I grabbed my leather jacket and bolted for the door. "Shit shit shit!"

"Don't sweat it," Luna said as I raced out to my black Toyota Highlander parked on the street. "It's not like you'll be late for a meeting with the queens of the world or something."

I was totally frazzled and out of breath when I threw open the door of Doc Yough's Bar and Grill, fifteen minutes late for my meeting with the Earth Mothers.

Seated around a table in the middle of the place, they all looked my way when the door burst open. All I could do was wave and hope for the best.

The proprietor, Rune Ansel Carson, came to my rescue from behind the bar, reaching out to give me a welcoming hug. "Gaia!" A stocky young woman with shoulder-length green hair, Rune was a hardcore environmental activist and special Human Liaison to the Council of Landkind. She'd helped in the war against the alien Allself and the Terralyzers, then taken over Doc Yough's after its former owner, Mahoney Wells, died in that very same war. Given her work with Landkind, and the fact that Doc Yough's was a major Landkind hangout, it could not have been a more perfect arrangement.

"Sorry I'm late," I said as the hug ended. "I got tied up at the office and lost track of—"

"Your timing is perfect." Rune guided me by the elbow to the big table. "The Mothers were just talking about a new outreach program to find the next generation of avatars."

"That's right!" Maeve, who sat at the side of the table nearest me, grinned and nodded. "With so many Earth Mothers instead of just one, we need more Earth/human avatars than ever…especially given our aggressive zero-pollution initiative."

Drusilla, who was seated at the far side of the table, nodded in agreement. "Since, technically, you're the only currently active avatar, we thought you'd be perfect to search, recruit, train, and educate."

"I can't think of anyone who'd do a better job of it." Mid, sitting between them, beamed and pointed a finger in my direction. "If you ask me, you're a natural, dear."

I couldn't help smiling back at them. Thanks to the infusion of True Mother's power, they looked healthier and more youthful than ever. Not to mention, they were all smartly dressed in colorful summer outfits; it hadn't taken them long, after returning from the Earth's core to reclaim their physical bodies, to do away with the plain white shifts.

"What do you say, Gaia?" asked Maeve. "Are you up to the task?"

"Maybe," I said. "As long as it doesn't interfere with my own work, taking on eco-crime cases and harassing polluters. I swore I'd never drop the ball again when it comes to the war for survival."

"That is definitely our number one priority." Drusilla nodded. "The clock is ticking. Time is running out."

"Faster than you know." Maeve raised her eyebrows. "*Much* faster."

I frowned. "What are you talking about?"

"You remember I said there are factions in the Ancestrum?" said Maeve.

I nodded.

"Not everyone among us wanted humanity to survive," continued Maeve. "And those women didn't suddenly change their minds when they became Earth Mothers. If anything, they've gotten more vocal about it."

"Let's just say there are rumblings," said Drusilla. "Not from everyone, but still…"

"More than enough to light the fuse," said Mid. "And eventually, blow the whole thing to kingdom come."

"With humankind first on the chopping block," added Maeve.

My frown deepened. "This is starting to sound like a civil war."

Drusilla threw her hands up, palms facing outward. "Nobody's saying that."

"*Yet*," said Mid.

"So you see why it's more important than ever to keep the humans in check?" asked Maeve. "To make sure they don't give the anti-human faction fuel for the fire?"

"Okay." I paused. "Then what you're saying is, we need to come down hard on humanity for pollution, because if we don't, the anti-human faction will come down *too* hard?"

"Basically," said Mid. "And we need to be ready for a surprise civil war among the Earth Mothers at any time."

"Which could tear the world apart as effectively as humankind," said Maeve.

"Well, that's a relief." I pretended to wipe sweat from my forehead with the back of my hand. "Here I thought you were going to say there was something to *worry* about."

Everyone laughed at that except Drusilla.

"So, now you see why we need those new avatar recruits," said Maeve. "And having them be pro-humanity wouldn't be a bad thing."

"Relatively speaking, pro-humanity," said Mid. "Maybe anti-human-extinction would be a better way of putting it."

"While still being anti-pollution," agreed Drusilla. "Extremely so."

"You want to stack the deck," I said.

"Just a little," said Mid. "Just enough."

"Because you better believe *they* will do the same thing," said Maeve.

"All right then. I've already got a recruit for you." I turned and smiled at Rune. "And yes, I know in my heart she'll make a hell of an avatar."

Rune looked stunned. "Me? Are you serious?"

I looked at the Earth Mothers, and they all looked at each other, just as surprised as Rune seemed to be.

I didn't give them much time to raise an objection, though, before throwing my arm around Rune's shoulders. "So, how would you like to give your Earth-saving efforts some real *teeth?* Without wiping humankind from the face of the planet, that is."

Rune took off her dark-rimmed glasses with the coffee saucer lenses. At first, I thought she was just rubbing her eyes for effect, or because of irritation…but then I realized she was dealing with something else.

She didn't say a word to answer my question, but she didn't need to. Her vigorous nodding told us everything.

That, and the tears of joy overflowing from her eyes.

By the time I returned to Charmer Investigations, it was already dark out, and I was tired. The rest of the meeting at Doc Yough's had taken hours, as the Earth Mothers and I had discussed business, arranged for Rune's upgrade to avatar, and just enjoyed each other's company. In the end, there had been hugs all around and promises to get together soon and often in the interest of friendship as well as saving the world.

Now, all I wanted to do was check the office, go home, and go to bed.

Parking on the street, I saw the office was dark, but someone was loitering outside. Concerned, I hopped out of the Highlander, ready for action—and instantly relaxed. Two steps from the curb, I could make out who the loiterer was.

"Luna?" I approached her slowly.

She was craning her head to look up at the night sky, hands on her hips. "Hi, Gaia." She didn't sound happy. "How was your meeting?"

"What's going on, Luna?" I drew up beside her, apprehensive. "Are you okay?"

"See that?" She kept staring at a point in the sky.

Following her gaze, I saw the full moon hanging there, huge and white. "Your world," I said. "Sister of the Earth."

"Take a really good look," she told me. "Notice anything different about it?"

I squinted, searching for the difference she wanted me to see. "Should I?"

"Maybe not," said Luna. "But *I* do."

"What is it, then?" I asked.

Still, she kept her gaze glued on the moon. "It might not be visible to the naked eye yet. Most people won't feel the effects yet. But to me, it's practically *screaming*. I'm the moon's avatar, and it won't stop *screaming* in my head." Wincing, she reached up and rubbed her temples.

I still couldn't see any difference. "Screaming about what?"

"*Falling*, Gaia. The moon is *falling* toward the Earth. It's getting closer every second."

Hearing that, I felt a fresh cloud of dread pass over my soul. I'd just gone through hell in every possible way, and now *this?*

"What could be causing it?" I asked.

"I have no idea," said Luna, "but we need to do something."

"Like what?" I didn't even know where to start. Could the combined power of the Earth Mothers and Landkind have an impact?

"Only my people can stop this," she told me, "and they're up there, asleep." Still, her eyes were glued on the giant white disk in the sky. "Someone has to wake them up *soon*, or we'll *all* have the same nightmare."

"Meaning what?"

"Eventually, the moon will fall *all the way*," said Luna, "and *two* worlds will collide into *one.*"

Gazing up at the moon, I still wasn't sure it looked closer…but I trusted Luna. As the avatar of that long-dead little world, she knew it as intimately as I knew the Earth. She was the expert, and I knew better than to doubt or downplay what she told me…unfortunately.

I'd only just started getting back to normal, and I hadn't fully processed my situation with Briar or my feelings for Ebon (if any), and all I wanted to do was live and be calm for a while, enjoying the "smooth sailing" side of my bipolar existence…but based on what she'd told me, that wouldn't be possible. As usual, it was "sinking fast" all over again. Why did it always have to be "sinking fast?"

It was starting to feel like a curse.

"So, Luna," I said. "What can we do to wake your people from here?"

"Nothing." Finally, she looked down to meet my gaze. "Nothing from *here*."

"From where, then?" I knew the answer before I asked the question, and I didn't *want* to hear it, but I had to ask anyway. "Where do we have to go to wake them?"

Still holding my gaze, she slowly raised a finger and pointed at the full moon, which suddenly looked much bigger and more terrifying than it had ever before looked in my life.

Thank you for reading *World on Fire*, book four in the Gaia Files.

We hope you enjoyed it as much as we enjoyed bringing it to you. We just wanted to take a moment to encourage you to review the book on Amazon and Goodreads. Every review helps further the author's reach and, ultimately, helps them continue writing fantastic books for us all to enjoy.

If you liked this book, check out the rest of our catalogue at www.aethonbooks.com. To sign up to receive a FREE collection from some of our best authors as well as updates regarding all new releases, visit www.aethonbooks.com/sign-up.

JOIN THE STREET TEAM! Get advanced copies of all our books, plus other free stuff and help us put out hit after hit.

SEARCH ON FACEBOOK:
AETHON STREET TEAM